The Atlantis Secret

Book 4

The Atlantis Saga

S.A. Beck

ISBN-13: 978-1987859379
ISBN-10: 1987859375

Contents

Chapter 1

July 7, 2016, LOS ANGELES, CALIFORNIA

12:35 P.M.

Jaxon Ares Andersen was beginning to think she was finally getting a life—not a good life, not even a halfway decent life, but something that kinda sorta looked like a life.

And that was way better than anything she'd ever had before.

She and Brett Lawson, her one and only friend at summer school, were sitting at a picnic table under the shade of a palm tree during their lunch break.

Being the richest, snottiest school in Los Angeles, Hidden Hills Academy didn't have anything so gauche as a cafeteria. People brought their own meals or went to one of the fancy restaurants nearby. A couple kids even had lunch delivered by their chauffeurs. Jaxon's foster mother, Isadore Grant, had packed Jaxon her usual supply of rabbit food—salad with organic vegetables and sprouts, organic gluten-free yogurt, plus some wholegrain bread. At least her thermos had one of Isadore's epic smoothies. It was the only thing coming out of her kitchen that tasted good.

Jaxon kept reaching across the table to swipe Brett's Doritos or steal a sip of his Coke. She left his microwave hamburger and fries alone, though. A girl had to have some respect for her body.

"This is robbery," Brett said. "We're supposed to be the good guys, remember?"

Jaxon raised an eyebrow and looked Brett full in the face.

"Stop me," she said, grabbing some more Doritos.

Brett chuckled, his smile bringing out the dimples on both his cheeks. His blond hair flopped as he shook his head.

"No way. You're a better martial artist than me. It's those private lessons you get. Maybe I should get some too."

"Maybe you should take your hand off my thigh before I give you a personal lesson," Jaxon said.

Brett slid his hand away, running it down her leg and over her knee before pulling back.

"Sorry," he said, not sounding sorry at all. "I figured since you were sharing my lunch that meant we were an item."

"That is so middle school. No, we're not an item."

"But we're really good together. We always have fun at lunch, and we're cleaning up the city one bad guy at a time."

"I can't date the captain of the golf team. I'd never forgive myself."

Brett shrugged. "I'll give up golf."

"Yeah, right. Your parents would have a hissy fit."

Brett made a face. "True. Plus, I need it. It's a good skill to have. Lots of business connections are made on the green. You should try it."

"Boring. Rather watch paint dry."

"That's unfair."

"Unfair to paint?" she asked. "Probably."

"So what do you want to do this weekend?"

"Not sure. What about we get together tonight and talk about it?"

Brett's face darkened. "I don't know."

He looked as though he was about to say something more when a shrill, snide female voice interrupted him.

"Well the eyes are pretty, but the rest is a mess!"

Jaxon and Brett turned although they already knew who it was.

Courtney, the class bully and the snobbiest kid in the snobbiest school in the state, was also the class cocaine dealer. At Hidden Hills, that guaranteed her popularity. She was tall, almost six feet, with long blond hair, blue eyes, and a fine figure enhanced by designer clothing. Jaxon suspected that pert little nose had been enhanced by surgery— she wouldn't have minded enhancing it further with her fist.

Courtney stood at the front of a little crowd of giggling admirers, studying Jaxon. "Yeah, really pretty eyes. You hardly ever see eyes that blue, even in Sweden. We go to Sweden a lot. My uncle is CEO of Ikea, so we like to visit his country home. It's so nice to escape the heat. But how did a mongrel like her get eyes like that?"

"She probably stole them. That's what her kind do," one of her followers said.

"Her kind" echoed in Jaxon's mind. There it was. Someone always had to point out that she was the only black-skinned person in the class. The only other minority was the son of some Japanese millionaire there for a year on business. Jaxon felt lucky, though. She'd been spending time in the exclusive neighborhood for a couple of months, and no cop had shot her yet.

Courtney went on as though the girl hadn't said anything. She never acknowledged anything anyone said unless it was a compliment aimed at her. "So weird to see those pretty eyes on such an ugly face—ugly black skin like she's straight from the ghetto and a flat face like she's from some Indian reservation. We got Frankenstein in our class."

"Frankenstein's monster," Jaxon said, her face flushing with anger.

Courtney gave her a blank look, a common expression for her. "Huh?"

"Frankenstein's monster," Jaxon repeated. "Frankenstein was the doctor who made the monster."

Courtney frowned. "What the hell are you talking about?"

"The book. You've never seen the movie?"

There had been a kid in one of Jaxon's group homes who loved classic horror movies. Jaxon had watched them with him on Saturday nights since she had nothing else to do. What was his name again? Didn't matter. Just another potential friend taken away as the system shuffled her and the rest of the unwanted kids around like cards in some bureaucratic poker game.

"No, I've never seen the movie, you nerd," Courtney said. "Why would I?"

"So that you don't sound like an idiot when you talk about it?"

That got a couple of titters from the crowd. Jaxon smiled. She was getting better at fending off airheads like Courtney.

"Watch it, ugly duckling," Courtney snapped.

"That's from a book," Jaxon said, "and I'm sure you haven't read it because you never read. Oh, by the way, the ugly duckling turned into a swan when it grew up."

Jaxon tensed as she realized her mistake. She shouldn't have brought up reading. That left Courtney an opening, and the girl saw it immediately.

"Yeah, like you can read. You sound like a total retard in class."

Jaxon flushed, grateful that her dark skin kept people from seeing it.

Dyslexia. It's called dyslexia, and a lot of people have it. It doesn't mean I'm stupid. She didn't say anything, though. She felt too ashamed.

As Jaxon fumed, Courtney turned to Brett. "I don't know why you hang out with this spaz."

"She's fun, and she isn't a cokehead," he said.

Courtney sneered at him. "You used to be cool."

"You used to be sober. Oh wait, that was fifth grade."

"So when did you guys start sleeping together?" Courtney asked.

"We're not," Brett and Jaxon said at the same time.

"Wow, Brett, that was a quick denial! Sounds like someone's covering up or maybe too embarrassed to admit they're bagging an ugly duckling like her. Hey, ugly duckling, keep him looking at your eyes—they're the only attractive part of you. Better not lose them."

Without warning, Courtney jabbed her long, manicured nails at Jaxon's eyes. Jaxon whipped a hand up and pinched hard on the pressure point between Courtney's thumb and forefinger.

"Ow! Watch it," the bully cried, yanking her hand away and shaking it to kill the pain. She glared at Brett. "Get some taste or you'll end up a loser like her."

With that, she spun around and frumped off, her gaggle of followers trailing behind. A couple looked over their shoulders in wonder at Jaxon.

"Nice move," Brett said.

Jaxon didn't reply. Her hands were shaking, and she was seeing red. She could go toe to toe with a gang member in a dark alley, but a classmate making fun of her always left her in pieces.

"You okay?" Brett asked.

"Let's go out again tonight," Jaxon said, hearing her voice come out weak, pleading.

Brett sat back, exhaling slowly. "Remember what happened last time?"

They'd been out on one of their nighttime crime-fighting hunts when they had bumped into some guy who tried to steal Brett's Porsche. The guy had pulled a gun. Jaxon had managed to disarm him, but the incident had freaked them both out. That had been a week before, and they hadn't gone on any night adventures since.

"We'll be careful," Jaxon said.

"We were careful last time. You can't avoid trouble if it comes to get you."

"Come on, we'll be fine. I need it."

She did need it. Walking the streets at night and looking for trouble made her feel alive. Her foster parents were clueless, and she could slip out of the house easily. She'd done it more than a dozen times.

Once out in Los Angeles at night, she felt like a completely different person— free, confident, useful. The first time she'd gone out on one of her nighttime walks, she had been in her own neighborhood and had stopped two of her neighbors from roughing up a prostitute. She wasn't even looking for trouble—she just wanted to get some air—but that first experience got her hooked. The prostitute was grateful, and when she mentioned she'd been in a group home like Jaxon, something clicked.

There was a city full of lost people out there, being victimized by sharks masquerading as human beings. That first experience just a few doors down from the Grants' mansion had woken Jaxon up to her potential.

After that, she gradually increased her range, getting out of her privileged little cul-de-sac and venturing into rougher and rougher neighborhoods. She stopped several muggings and saved a couple of girls from getting assaulted.

Brett was right, of course—trouble did have a way of finding her. It had been that way all her life. The only thing that changed was that instead of hiding in her shell hoping it would pass her by, now she encouraged it. A lone sixteen-year-old girl in a bad part of town was a magnet that pulled in all sorts of bad characters.

That was the point. You couldn't tell bad from good just by looking at someone, so you had to get the bad ones to come to you. And then you punished them.

Jaxon nearly had a heart attack when she stumbled upon Brett doing the same thing. Like her, he felt lonely and out of place in the boring upper-class life he led, a life of golf resorts and airy cokeheads like Courtney. His parents lived with him, but they were almost as distant as the parents Jaxon had never known.

So she and Brett teamed up, looking for trouble in some of the worst areas of the city, with Jaxon as the bait.

It was a crazy thing to do, dumb even by Brett's standards, yet they kept on going back to it like a favorite drug. She loved the thrill, the secrecy, the danger. Also, she loved the fact that she got to do some good with her life. They saved a lot of people from being robbed or worse.

Plus she liked the simplicity of it. On the streets, some thug could come up to her, and she could simply beat him up. Someone like Courtney turning the class against her and laughing at her skin color, what did Jaxon do about that? She couldn't hit her no matter how much she wanted to.

Jaxon had been thrown out of enough schools for stunts like that, and she didn't want to get thrown out of another one. She had an okay thing with the Grants. As far as foster parents went, they ranked pretty high. Stephen never stared at her boobs, and they didn't try to convert her to some hardcore brand of religion. And neither of them got all condescending like some white foster parents did, like Jaxon should be eternally grateful that her Great White Saviors had consented to have an unwanted "colored girl" in the house. She'd had more than a few foster families like that. She had to hand it to Courtney—at least she was honest about her racism.

So yeah, Jaxon had a decent thing going. Sure, Isadore's hippie food was nasty, but Jaxon got to live in a mansion and had private martial-arts and yoga lessons. Plus, she had the doofus across the table as a friend. The Grants said they'd keep her until she went to college, which was two years away. She'd never lived in one place that long in her entire life.

Having a bit of a life felt nice, and tasting what life was like made her want to taste even more.

Brett was still sitting there, looking at her dubiously. She could tell he'd been following her thoughts.

"I really think we should cool off for a while," he said. "We could have gotten killed."

"Please?"

He inclined his head and sighed. Jaxon felt a spike of guilt. That incident with the gun had really shaken him up. To her surprise, she didn't feel the same. In fact, it made her want to go out even more. Sure, she had been so scared at the time that she had almost peed herself, yet she wanted to go out again more than ever.

The bell rang, signaling the time to go back to class.

"Please, Brett?"

He looked up and grinned at her. "It is pretty fun, huh?"

Jaxon laughed. "Much better than that stuff Courtney snorts up her nose, not that I'd know."

"Oh, trust me, it's way better than that stuff."

Jaxon rolled her eyes. "Oh God, don't tell me how you know that. So I'll meet you at the end of my street at 10:00 p.m.?"

Brett hesitated.

"Come on, please?"

"I don't know. I have a bad feeling about this." He glanced at the students filing into the building. "We'll talk after class."

"No way. Isadore will swoop down and whisk me away to some lesson, and you know she never lets me use the phone. We have to plan it now."

"I just think we're pushing our luck."

"Please?" she asked.

Brett sighed. "Okay, but we have to be careful, understand?"

"Thanks!" Jaxon jumped up and gave him a hug across the table.

"Oh, hey, if you put it that way, we can—"

Jaxon clamped a hand over his mouth. "Don't say anything lame. In other words, don't say anything at all."

She pulled her hand away and picked up her book bag.

Brett stood and gave her a mock bow. "I only said yes because I knew you'd go out there without me if I said no. I wouldn't want that. You need someone to protect you."

Jaxon wagged a finger at him. "That's the dumbest thing you've said all day."

Chapter 2

JULY 7, 2016, SONORA DESERT,
55 MILES SOUTHWEST OF TUCSON,
ARIZONA

12:35 P.M.

If there was one thing Otto Heike had learned in his time as part of the Atlantis Allegiance, it was that getting shot at really sucked.

It wasn't so much the "a high-speed chunk of steel could rip through my body at any moment" part or even the little fact that he could wind up dead in the next few seconds, it was more the nastiness of it all. A group of strangers were doing their best to kill him and his friends for no other reason than wanting to stop Otto from rescuing his girlfriend and making what would be the biggest historical discovery since King Tut's tomb. Those people figured that since they had larger numbers and more guns, they could tell the Atlantis Allegiance to do whatever they wanted.

Like dying.

It was bullying pure and simple, Otto thought as a burst of semiautomatic rounds chewed up the windowsill through which he was trying to peek outside, spitting bits of concrete into his face. He had never liked bullies.

The only way to deal with bullies was to fight back.

Otto waited until the burst finished, and he popped up from the windowsill just enough to level his grenade launcher, pull the trigger, and lob a round across the overgrown parking lot to hit the cracked pavement right in front of the three black sedans parked nose to nose like a wall a hundred yards away.

Otto ducked just as another bullet whizzed through the window to smack into the back wall of the abandoned gas station where the government agents had him cornered. A moment later, there was a flash and a boom outside.

"Good shot, Pyro!" Grunt said beside him. The hulking mercenary popped up to spray the cars with bullets from his machine gun then ducked down again to avoid any return fire. "Looks like you dazzled a few. Wind's too strong to keep the smoke blocking their line of fire, though. Launch another, and maybe we'll get a chance to get out of here."

"It would help if you gave me real grenades instead of flash-and-smoke bombs!" Otto shouted as he reloaded.

"You want to kill people?"

"No, but it looks like a lot of people want to kill me!"

Otto had been on the run ever since the little band of mercenaries had sprung him from jail. At times, things calmed down, like a week ago when they'd spent a relaxing night in Tucson, eating Mexican food and learning about the Atlanteans from an old professor. But those guys in black suits, the government agents sent by General Meade, had located them again, cornering them in an old, crumbling gas station on a back county road.

The agents had picked their spot well. All around the gas station stretched a vast, flat desert of rock and cacti. There was nobody for miles, not even a ranch house. The Atlantis Allegiance always drove the back roads to avoid getting sighted. That worked most of the time, but whenever they got attacked, they couldn't hope for any help.

It was just Otto, Grunt, and the half-dozen government agents outside.

"When's Vivian getting here?" Otto shouted over the sound of gunfire.

"ETA one minute," Grunt shouted back.

More shots stitched a pattern into the back wall. Otto crawled to the next window over, kicking some old beer cans out of his path. Keep moving and keep them guessing. Grunt had taught him that. The building looked like it got used frequently as a local party place. Graffiti decorated some of the walls, and empty cans and cigarette stubs littered the floor. At least the partiers had broken all the windows already. If they hadn't, Grunt and Otto would be getting showers of glass. Those agents' aim was far too good for Otto's comfort.

Vivian and Dr. Yamazaki had driven off to open a cache of equipment hidden down the road while he and Grunt stayed at the station to open up a second cache containing some electronic supplies Edward needed. The agents arrived a minute after Vivian had driven out of sight. Otto hoped they hadn't sent a second group after her. Getting saved by Vivian was Plans A, B, and C.

There was no Plan D.

At least Edward and Dr. Yuhle were a hundred miles away with the trailer. No way they'd get that lumbering vehicle out of the mess Otto was in. It went from zero to sixty in about five hours.

"Outgoing!" Otto shouted, popping up and firing the grenade launcher. He barely made it back out of sight before a bullet cracked off the windowsill.

A moment later, a flash and a thud told him his grenade had gone off. A second after that, a deep boom shook the entire building. The back wall of the gas station was illuminated in garish red.

"Damn, Pyro, you hit one of their gas tanks!" Grunt shouted.

Otto dared a peek outside. A mushroom cloud of flame billowed up from one of the sedans. The haze of smoke from his last bomb shrouded the whole area, weirdly backlit by the burning car. Agents scampered off in all directions to avoid the flames. For a brief second, Otto felt relieved no one had gotten incinerated, but his thoughts were soon swept away by the beautiful sight of the flames.

Otto stared at the mushroom cloud as it dissipated twenty feet above the parking lot before his gaze drifted back down to the car. The entire vehicle was aflame, the biggest fire coming from the engine, the flames reaching higher and higher as oil and rubber lit. The initial boom, he realized, had been the gas tank exploding. He'd have to remember that. It was gorgeous.

A screech of tires snapped him out of his daze and made him look to the right. A red Subaru Impreza swerved into the parking lot, the driver's window open with an Uzi's muzzle pointing out and flaring with gunfire.

"About time she got here!" Grunt shouted. "I hate waiting on women, especially when I'm getting shot at. You ready to run, Pyro?"

"If it means getting out of here, you can bet on it."

The Subaru squealed to a stop in front of the gas station. Otto grabbed the duffel bag full of gear they'd dug up in the backyard and hurried out the front door as Grunt provided cover fire.

Vivian popped open the back seat, and he dove right in. A second later, he had the wind knocked out of him as Grunt landed on top of him.

"Sorry, Pyro." Grunt rolled off of him and slammed the door.

"You boys have fun while I was gone?" Vivian asked, slamming on the gas and swerving the car around, making Otto fly to one side and bounce off of the wall of muscle that was Grunt.

"Otto's getting good with that grenade launcher," Grunt said, slapping a full magazine into his Uzi. "He's figured out how to blow up a car."

Despite the danger, Otto felt a flush of shame. For years, he'd struggled with his addiction to lighting fires, and now he had to do it to stay alive.

But stay alive for how long? Otto looked out the back window as the gas station dwindled in the distance. Already, the agents were getting back together. One of the sedans pulled away from the fire.

Dr. Yamazaki popped up in the passenger's seat beside Vivian. She'd been hiding below the dashboard.

"Oh, there you are," Grunt said in a cheerful tone.

The geneticist stared at him, her face pale. She was even more overwhelmed by all this than Otto was.

"They're coming after us," Otto said.

"Of course they are, honey," Vivian said. "These guys never give up. Wonder how they found us this time."

"Maybe someone hacked into Edward's communications," Otto said.

Grunt shook his head, the sweat glistening on the tribal tattoo covering most of his shaven scalp. "No one hacks Edward. Maybe they traced the Tohono O'odham. They're careful but not as trained as we are. Someone might have slipped up."

"I told you we shouldn't have helped them trash that uranium mine!" Otto said.

The mercenary rounded on him. "Fighting General Meade isn't the only war we're in, Pyro!"

Otto glared back at him. "You busted me out of jail to save Jaxon, and all we've been doing is running around the desert for the past few weeks getting shot at!"

"We'll get your girlfriend when we can, kid. Right now, we've got more pressing problems."

Vivian chimed in from the front seat. "Um, boys? Perhaps you should stop arguing and see what our friends are up to?"

Grunt and Otto turned around in their seat to look behind them. The highway was empty. They looked at each other.

"That's too good to be true," Otto said.

Grunt craned his neck, looking out the window into the sky.

"What are you looking at?" Otto asked.

"Thought I spotted something. Damn, there it is. A drone!"

"What! Where?"

Grunt pointed. "There."

Otto spotted a small black X silhouetted against the bright desert sky. "Vivian, start weaving. It's going to shoot a missile at us!"

"Relax, Pyro," Grunt said. "It's just an observation drone. It's too small to carry ordnance. It will keep after us, though. If we don't shoot it down, we'll never shake those guys. That thing's got a camera they're monitoring. They're probably hanging back, waiting for reinforcements."

Grunt rolled down the window, pulled a rifle out from behind the seat, and lifted himself partway out the window.

"Hold onto me, Pyro."

Otto grabbed him around the waist. Vivian didn't slow down. They must have been going eighty.

"Watch those hands, Pyro. I'm not phobic, but when I was in the service, the rule was 'Don't ask, don't tell.'"

"Shut up and shoot that drone!" Otto shouted.

Otto would have never shouted at someone who looked like Grunt until a few weeks before. He'd never handled a grenade launcher either. A lot had changed in his life.

The sound of a high-powered rifle shooting next to his head slammed his eardrums. Grunt fired twice more. Otto craned his head and saw the drone plummeting to earth. The mercenary wormed his way back inside the vehicle.

"I hate drones," Grunt said as he thumped back into his seat. "Damn things kill innocent people all around the world while their pilots sit back at base, thinking they're playing some damn video game."

"They only use them to kill terrorists," Otto said.

Grunt snorted. "You keep telling yourself that, Pollyanna."

"Now what?" Otto asked, peering up into the sky to search for more drones.

"Now we get out of here as fast as we can, ditch this Subaru, and grab another vehicle they won't recognize, honey," Vivian said from the front seat.

"But where will we get one?"

"Where do you think?" Grunt asked. "We'll steal one."

Otto threw up his hands. "Whoa! Wait a minute. I'm not a thief, and don't pull that 'Yeah, but you're a pyromaniac' line on me. Just because I've done some bad things in my life doesn't mean I have to keep on doing more bad stuff."

"If you don't help us steal a car, you'll be aiding and abetting a murder."

"Whose?"

"Our own."

Otto paused, trying to think of a way around that but came up with nothing.

"There's got to be a better way," he said, his voice lacking conviction.

"Wish there was, honey," Vivian said. "But there isn't. If they have one drone, they'll have another. Let's grab the first car we can, something fast and expensive. That way, the owner will be sure to have theft insurance. We'll ditch it as soon as we can, and then the cops will collect it and give it back. Sure, we'll be ruining someone's day, but we'll be saving our own lives."

Grunt punched him in the shoulder. Just a playful punch. A real punch would have shot Otto through the door.

"Consider it a math lesson," the mercenary said. "You gotta do a lot of math in this game. Here's an equation for you. Are four lives greater than, equal to, or less than the value of one civilian's ruined day? Hell, even if his car ends up getting trashed, four lives is greater than the value of one civilian's car, right?"

Otto sank back in his seat and closed his eyes. Being with the crew meant he was always on the run. Back in California, he was wanted for a prison break, not to mention the false charge of setting fire to the greenhouse at his group home. The one fire he hadn't set was the one he got tried as an adult for. Just his luck.

"I still don't like it," Otto grumbled.

Grunt put a beefy hand on his shoulder, and Otto turned to him.

"Good. I don't want you to like it. You're not a bad kid for a pyro, and I don't want all this drama to turn you bad."

Otto caught a look of pain in Grunt's eyes, quickly hidden. Something had happened when he had been in the Special

Forces, something Grunt only hinted at. Whatever that was, it meant he would leave the Atlantis Allegiance once they saved Jaxon. As soon as Dr. Yamazaki and her old professor Dr. Charles Smith had decided they needed to go to Morocco to hunt down the original Atlanteans, Grunt had told them he was out.

Whatever Grunt had experienced in North Africa, he didn't want to face it again.

Otto looked at him out of the corner of his eye. As annoying as the guy was, he didn't want the mercenary to leave. Grunt wasn't a bad guy, and Otto had a feeling that if they really did get Jaxon away from Meade's people and ran all the way to Morocco, that wouldn't get them out of danger.

No, Otto thought as he put another flash-and-smoke bomb into his grenade launcher, *the danger is just beginning.*

Chapter 3

JULY 7, 2016, LOS ANGELES,
CALIFORNIA
10:05 P.M.

The sounds of the night surrounded Jaxon as she stood in the shadow of a tree near the end of her street. That was always the most peaceful part of her day, waiting alone outside for Brett to pick her up.

As usual, her foster parents didn't suspect a thing. Stephen and Isadore Grant went to bed early and never checked on her at night, plus the lawn below her window was thick grass and soft soil. Jumping down made almost no sound. Even though her room was on the second floor above a high-ceilinged living room, the jump felt like stepping off a chair. Jaxon had unnaturally good strength and agility, and her knees barely bent when she landed from the twenty-foot fall.

If only my mind was as strong and as quick as my body.

Courtney's jokes from lunchtime were still bothering her. Bullies made her want to curl up and blow away. It was so much easier when they physically attacked her because then she could hit them.

Maybe this isn't the best way to deal with that problem.

She suppressed the thought as soon as it came up. It sounded like all the social workers and psychologists she had ever had. Easy for them to talk, none of them had been shuffled from foster home to group home and back again two or three times a year. They'd all grown up with loving parents in happy homes.

Jaxon knew that for a fact. She'd asked every single one of them.

No, the little adventures in the crappy parts of LA were good for her. She'd never felt so confident before, and being out put to good use all that aikido practice she'd been doing with her instructor, Marquis. She'd stopped dozens of crimes.

The low rev of Brett's Porsche caught her attention. He drove slowly and stopped a little past the tree under which she was hiding. She kept behind the trunk so she didn't get caught in the headlights.

Once the lights were shining farther down the road, she hurried over and got into the car, keeping to the shadows as much as possible. Hers was a quiet neighborhood, but there still might be eyes watching, especially that pervy neighbor she'd had to stop from beating up that prostitute.

"You ready?" She buckled up as Brett turned the car around.

"I was born ready, baby," he said, giving her that stupid grin of his.

"Lame."

"What? It's original."

"No, it's not original."

"No?"

"No."

He looked sidelong at her. "How about, 'You're the only friend I have worth having?' Is that original?"

Something inside Jaxon shifted. No one had ever said that to her before. Otto had said all sorts of nice things to her during the few precious weeks he'd been her boyfriend, but he'd been a messed-up kid sharing a group home with her. Brett was a popular rich kid, deliberately losing his popularity to hang out with her and take her side in arguments.

She glanced at him and caught him looking at her. Why didn't she give him a chance? He was a bit of a dork, and the golfing thing had to go, but he was cute and kind.

Was she still holding a torch for Otto? She guessed she was. He'd been her first boyfriend, and she had needed some time to admit to herself that she'd never see him again—maybe she should move on.

"Ah, you've gone all quiet!" Brett said. "My charm stuns all the girls into silence."

She broke out in laughter. "I knew you were going to ruin it by saying something dumb!"

But he hadn't ruined it. Even his dumbness had become charming.

Brett stared at her, a wide smile deepening the dimples on either side of his mouth.

"Watch the road," Jaxon said.

Brett chuckled and turned back to look where they were going. He'd gotten onto an access road to the highway, where there were plenty of cheap bars and motels. There'd be good hunting here.

After a moment, he spoke, quietly and thoughtfully, as if he'd practiced what he wanted to say.

"It's just that everything is more real with you, Jaxon. Even when we're just goofing off, eating lunch, you say stuff that makes sense. You're way smarter than most people I know, and you're pretty too. Oh, don't go rolling your eyes. You always do that when I say you're good looking, but you are. You're good looking in a different way. It's like you're a combination of all the best features of all the different races. Too bad you don't know your parents—I bet they have a ton of stories to tell. Don't be too hard on them for leaving you. They might have had good reasons. It's better not to have parents than parents who don't want you. But what I'm trying to say, Jaxon, is that it doesn't matter if you want to go out with me or not. I've really loved these lunches and the crazy stuff we're doing right now. I want you to remember that. This won't last, you know, and I want you to remember that."

Jaxon didn't know what to say, so she said nothing. They drove in silence for a while, Jaxon looking straight ahead, not daring to turn to see if Brett was looking at her.

Brett slowed the Porsche as they passed a strip mall containing a bar, an all-night liquor store, a few cheap shops all closed and shuttered, and a run-down motel with a garish neon sign from the sixties, which offered hourly rates. Beyond that, Jaxon spotted the dim lights of a cheap housing development.

Jaxon felt a mixture of familiarity, guilt, and disgust. She'd lived in a few neighborhoods like that herself. She knew how they could be.

"Pull in here," she said in a soft voice.

Her emotions from a moment before got drowned out by the electric thrill of the hunt. It wouldn't be long before they faced danger again, stopping some innocent person from getting hurt or drawing out some robber or perv who deserved to be punished.

In the back of her mind, Jaxon knew that this was just some coping mechanism for all her problems. She'd been talking to psychologists and stuck in group therapy with basket-case kids all her life. She knew all the tricks the mind could play. Jaxon felt powerless and awkward in her regular life, the life where she had to obey the rules and had to deal with people who knew her.

Out here, she faced a different reality. She could be whoever she wanted to be. Nobody had any preconceptions of her, and the rules were simple—win or lose. Losing wasn't an option when she considered just how badly she'd get hurt.

There was another level to it, though, one none of her shrinks could ever guess—here she could reveal some of her extraordinary powers. She looked like a petite teenage girl, just five foot three and one hundred twenty pounds, yet she was stronger than an adult weightlifter and as fast as Bolt, and thanks to her martial-arts training, she had become one of the best fighters she'd ever seen. She had to pull her punches with her triple-black-belt instructor just to keep him from catching on. These adventures were no real danger to her, even when she had to pull back on her abilities to keep Brett from thinking she was some sort of mutant. She'd never told him about her powers and figured he thought she was just some martial-arts prodigy.

If he only knew! Imagine his face if I showed him I can sometimes move objects with my mind. She looked at his handsome features in the streetlight streaming through the windshield.

His eyes roved from side to side, brow furrowed in concentration.

No, that would freak him out. Heck, it freaks me out. What am I, anyway?

Brett drove his Porsche down the length of the strip mall. Someone lay passed out on the sidewalk, his pockets turned inside out. Nearby, a man in a ragged overcoat staggered out of the all-night liquor store carrying a plastic bag. He lifted out a forty-ounce bottle of malt liquor, unscrewed the cap, and chugged it.

Moving slowly past the darkened façades of several stores, the fronts tagged with spray paint and the sidewalk littered with empty bottles and other trash, Brett and Jaxon approached the bar. A group of men in leather jackets stood in a loud, laughing circle, obviously drunk.

Brett slowed. A couple of the men stared, but nothing happened. Brett passed them and sped up, loping around to pass them again. One of the men gave them the finger.

Brett chuckled.

"How couldn't you want to go out with me when I always take you to such classy places?"

"Well, you do know how to show a girl a good time. Pull in down the road there between the bar and the pawn shop."

"Looks dark and crappy," Brett said, a strange edge to his voice.

"That's what we want, isn't it?"

"Well, yeah, but..."

Brett slowed the car almost to a stop. They hadn't yet turned into the darkened street. Jaxon turned to him in frustration.

"What's the matter with you tonight?"

"I just have a bad feeling—"

A woman's scream cut him off. Brett revved the engine, moved into the deep shadow beside the pawn shop, and stopped. In the brief moment before he switched off the lights, Jaxon saw a circle of figures about a block down the side road. Jaxon and Brett leapt out of the car, closing the doors quickly to cut off the car's interior light.

They paused, letting their eyes adjust. They stood in the alley, the sides blocked by the bare concrete walls of the pawn shop and the bar. The raucous conversation of the drunks echoed outside the bar behind them. In front, the alley opened up into an intersection with a couple of run-down houses on the corners. Another block farther on, past darkened homes and a couple of abandoned lots, stood the circle of figures they'd spotted.

Jaxon blinked. That far? Had the scream really come from there? It must have been loud, a scream of sheer terror.

And she and Brett were the only two people who had come to check it out.

They had difficulty seeing. No lights shone in the alley, and the nearest two streetlights were broken. The closest light flickered from a streetlight half a block away from the circle of figures. The figures were shifting. Something was going on over there.

Another scream tore the night air.

Jaxon felt sure the scream came from that group.

Without exchanging a word, Brett and Jaxon moved forward, spreading out to give each other room to fight. Brett was good with karate and had the strength and speed of a varsity athlete.

And Jaxon? Well, Jaxon was Jaxon.

Jaxon felt the warm rush of adrenaline flow through her veins. No doubts, no insecurities, no flailing around to find the right words to say to make people like her—it was just her and her friend against the bad guys.

And as they approached the crowd, Jaxon saw just how bad they were.

Jaxon counted a dozen of them, and at first she was surprised to see they all looked to be high-school age. Briefly, she wondered why they weren't at home in bed, but then she realized they'd come out looking for some fun, just as she had.

The center of the circle held their idea of fun.

A terrified girl, no more than fifteen, clutched at her torn shirt. Her jacket lay in a crumpled heap on the sidewalk. The guys all leered at her and made crude jokes.

Jaxon realized those sickos planned on attacking her right there on the sidewalk of a residential neighborhood.

They knew they were safe. No one would come running to investigate a girl's scream in that neighborhood.

No one, that is, except Brett and Jaxon.

The two friends picked up the pace, closing the distance between them and the sickos. Jaxon curled her lip in disgust at the designer shoes and labels the boys wore. They were rich kids slumming in a bad part of town in order to find what they wanted without having to worry about angry victims who could hire private investigators and lawyers. Jaxon had lived in enough poor neighborhoods to know that an attack like that would barely be investigated.

They made it to within fifty yards before any of the boys even noticed them.

"Hey, look, fresh meat!" one said.

The other boys turned.

Between two of them, Jaxon locked eyes with the terrified girl. "Don't worry," Jaxon called out to her. "We'll get you out of this."

Jaxon was amazed to hear the strength and confidence in her own voice. Why couldn't she sound like that in her normal life?

"Turn her over to us, and you won't get hurt," Brett said, an unexpected quaver in his voice.

What was wrong with him tonight?

One of the guys gave him a smug smile. "Funny, I was about to say the same to you."

The punk turned and looked Jaxon up and down. "Not bad. Want to have some fun?"

Great. Besides Brett, the only guy who wants me is this pervert.

"Yeah, I'd like to have some fun," Jaxon said, striding up to him as his friends chuckled.

Jaxon gave him a straight kick to the solar plexus—nothing fancy but effective enough. The air gushed out of his lungs with a whoosh, and he flew backward to land hard on the pavement.

Out of the corner of her eye, Jaxon spotted a dark shape rushing her. She spun, throwing a roundhouse kick. The guy saw it at the last second and ducked back, bringing his hands up to protect his face.

Jaxon ended up kicking him in the hand, which made him spin around and slap the guy next to him across the face. Both stumbled away.

That was a new one. Marquis would be proud of me.

Brett dove into the fight, then Jaxon had time to look only at what was coming right at her.

There were so many! The teens came at her all at once from all directions, obviously used to ganging up on people.

They probably came joyriding through poor neighborhoods all the time looking for someone to pick on.

They were picking on the wrong person.

Jaxon became a flurry of martial-arts moves. She didn't try to hold back. She didn't dare. She spun low, ducking under a punch that would have cracked a few of her teeth, extending her leg to sweep an arc that knocked the feet out from under two of her opponents. Then she leapt and spun to give an uppercut to a guy trying to grab her from behind. She didn't even get the satisfaction of seeing him fall because that instant, another fist came flying at her, and she had to flip the guy over her shoulder, conveniently hitting the next idiot diving toward her.

Through the melee, she spotted the girl being hustled away by three of her attackers. Jaxon busted through the crowd, knocking down anyone in her path, and cut them off.

The three guys snarled and pushed away their prey, who fell to the street, whimpering.

They spread out and approached Jaxon slowly. One came right at her while the other two edged toward her from the sides. Jaxon heard the thump of fists hitting flesh not far off. Brett sounded too busy to help her.

That was fine. Jaxon had been helping herself all her life.

As expected, the three attacked her all at once. They looked as though they had some training.

She ducked the first punch, barely blocked the second, and got the third right in her gut. It would have bent an ordinary girl double and left her tossing up the remains of her dinner.

An ordinary girl, but not Jaxon.

Hurt like hell, though.

Jaxon grabbed her opponent by the shirt and struck him in the head from one side while undercutting his opposite leg with her own. He flipped over sideways and hit the pavement with a loud thud. Jaxon spun and barely managed to block the guy to her left as he punched for her throat.

Her *throat*—a nasty technique Marquis had told her only to use if her life was in danger. Those guys didn't want to just hurt her. They wanted to do some real damage.

That got proven the next instant when she took a kick in the small of the back. The force of the blow pushed her into the grasp of the guy in front of her, who tried to pin her arms to her side.

Big mistake. It would have worked if she really was as weak as she looked. Instead, Jaxon whipped her arms up, breaking his hold. His arms splayed to the side, leaving him wide open for a direct hit to the face.

That put him down. Jaxon spun on her final attacker, only to get kicked again, that time in her side before she completed her move.

She absorbed the glancing blow with a grunt. Jaxon lashed out, smacking him in the face. She stepped forward to hit him again as he backpedaled, but she got tripped up by the guy on the ground, who was flailing about, trying to grab her.

A quick downward kick solved that problem, and a combination of blows finished off the problem standing in front of her. As he fell, she looked at him with a bit of respect. He'd blocked two of her strikes only to get downed by the third.

Martial arts are too popular in California. There's competition on these streets.

Jaxon looked around, suddenly aware that the street had gone silent.

The attackers were disappearing into the shadows in all four directions, leaving her alone with the girl. Most of the thugs had already left.

Brett was nowhere in sight.

"Brett?" she called out, peering down the darkened streets as the last of the teens limped away. "Brett!" she shouted at the top of her lungs.

She turned to the girl. "Did you see where my friend went?"

The girl shook her head. Her eyes were wet with tears and her cheeks streaked with mascara. She struggled to speak. "C-could you... take me home? It's not far."

With a last look around, Jaxon helped her up.

"This way." The girl paused to pick up her jacket.

Jaxon looked around again. "Brett! Where did he get to?"

"Thank you so much for helping me."

The girl shuffled down the road with Jaxon at her side.

"Could you speed it up a little?" Jaxon said impatiently. "Sorry, but I have to find my friend."

"I was coming home from the late shift at 7/11. I just got off the bus, and they jumped me. They were going to..." She broke down sobbing.

"It's all right now. You're safe." Jaxon rubbed her shoulder then looked around again. "Brett!"

"Please don't shout. They might come back."

"Are we at your house yet?" *This girl's taking forever just to walk down the street!*

"Just a little further."

"Where?" Jaxon hated to hurry the poor girl along, but she had to find Brett. He might still be fighting those guys somewhere. Beating them had been hard enough when she and Brett had been fighting side by side, and she didn't want to think what might happen if he was facing them all by himself.

The girl gestured vaguely down one of the side streets. Jaxon took her by the crook of the arm and hustled her that way.

"Please, they hurt my leg when they pushed me down." The girl started limping. She hadn't been limping before.

"Which one is your house?" Jaxon asked.

"The one at the end of the street."

Jaxon ground her teeth in frustration and pulled her along. The girl dragged her feet and limped more, which just made Jaxon's impatience grow.

Once they got a couple of doors away, Jaxon let her go. "Sorry I can't stick around. I have to find my friend."

"Couldn't you at least walk me to my door?" the girl asked.

"No. It's right there. I really have to go now."

"But—"

"Good night!" Jaxon growled and stalked off.

After she made it half a block, she felt guilty and turned around.

The girl was nowhere to be seen. No lights were on in her house.

Jaxon trotted back toward the girl's house but saw no sign of her or anyone else.

Must have left the lights off, afraid someone would know she was inside. I can't deal with her now. I have to find Brett!

She sprinted back to the scene of the fight. No one. Brett's Porsche still sat in the alley. Jaxon hurried over to it and found it untouched.

Damn, why couldn't she have a phone like everyone else in the world? Her foster parents had this weird idea of staying away from technology whenever possible and forbade her to have a phone except when she went out into the city alone, and of course they didn't know she was out right then.

She peeked her head around the corner to view the front of the strip mall. The drunk with the forty ounce sat slumped against a wall only a few feet away, mumbling something to himself. Only a couple of guys still stood in front of the bar, quietly smoking.

She called out to them and asked if they'd seen someone matching Brett's description.

"Sorry, babe, but if you're lonely..."

"Whatever." Jaxon sighed and turned back to the darkened neighborhood.

Where could he have gone? Think!

The guys had scattered in all directions. Could they have taken Brett with them? Or perhaps he chased some of them?

Jaxon had no idea. She jogged around the block, seeing nothing. Then she increased her search by a block and made another loop.

Still nothing.

She continued to search, a cold pit of fear growing in her stomach.

Chapter 4

July 8, 2016, LOS ANGELES,
CALIFORNIA
4:30 P.M.

Jaxon tried to stay awake as the science teacher droned on. She'd been up searching for Brett almost until dawn, fruitlessly running around that filthy neighborhood for any sign of him or their attackers. Several times, she returned to the Porsche, hoping he would be waiting for her there, but all she found was some guy trying to break into it. She gave him what he deserved, not that it made her feel any better.

At long last, she had to break off the search. It was past four in the morning, and her foster parents woke up ridiculously early. She got to a main road and hailed a cab. Since Stephen and Isadore were as stingy with pocket money as they were with her phone and Internet use, she only had enough to get partway home. She had to jog the last five miles as the sky to the east brightened from black to pink to pale blue.

She made it back home and climbed up to her room only minutes before hearing her foster parents moving around the house. She changed into her pajamas, slipped into her bed, and pretended to be asleep until Isadore came to wake her.

Jaxon managed to convince her to let her use her phone, claiming she had forgotten a homework assignment and needed to call a classmate. That got her a lecture, but at least it also got her the phone.

She called Brett. No answer. She texted him and held onto her phone for as long as she could. After breakfast, Isadore asked for it back, but she told her foster mother that she was still waiting for a reply. That managed to get her the phone until she had to leave for school. She almost burst into tears as she handed over her phone without having heard from Brett.

She was sick with worry by the time Isadore drove her to school. As soon as she got there, she rushed around the halls looking for him but didn't dare ask anyone. He wasn't in the student lounge or the tables outside or his homeroom. Nowhere.

Just before the class bell rang, she passed two kids she recognized from Brett's golf team and overheard one say to the other, "I called Brett's phone three times this morning and couldn't get him, and now it says it's switched off."

Jaxon's blood ran cold. She hovered nearby, hoping to get more information, but the two boys moved on to another subject, clueless about the real reason they couldn't get a hold of the captain of their team.

The rest of the day was a queasy blur. A few people commented on Brett's absence, but nobody thought to ask her. With Brett gone, she had turned invisible again.

To everyone but Courtney. The cokehead taunted her at lunch as usual, but Jaxon barely heard. She just stared off into the distance, wondering what had happened to her one and only friend in that horrible city while Courtney's insults just rolled off her unheard. Eventually, Courtney gave up, and Jaxon was left alone.

It wasn't until almost the end of the school day that the students heard anything. Before the final bell rang, the entire school got called into the auditorium.

The principal, Crystal Dennison, stood on stage, flanked by most of the teachers. They all looked somber. The golf coach, a big, beefy man in his sixties whose name Jaxon had never bothered to learn, was wiping his eyes. In a numb haze, Jaxon took a seat with the other kids.

After everyone was assembled, the principal stood up. The room fell silent. Ms. Dennison looked around at the kids and struggled to speak. Finally, she got the words out.

"I'm afraid I have some very bad news. One of our students, Brett Lawson, was found dead early this morning."

A gasp went through the room. Jaxon slumped in her seat. The whole room took on a distant, unreal quality. She felt as though she was watching a bad movie. The principal went on, her words sounding as if they were coming from the end of a long, echoing tunnel.

"He was found in a rough area of town about a mile from his car. He had been stabbed multiple times."

Jaxon winced, each word like the lash of a whip on her heart.

"It appears he was the victim of a mugging. The police are investigating. What they're trying to clear up right now is why Brett was walking in that neighborhood at that hour. It's miles from his home. If anyone talked to Brett or knows anything about this, I'd ask them to please come to see me or any other teacher you feel comfortable with after assembly. Any bit of information, even if you feel it's unimportant or not related to what happened, might help the police in their investigation and bring justice to Brett's... murderers." The last word came out choked.

The room remained silent except for a few scattered sobs.

After taking a moment to recover, Ms. Dennison said, "Brett Lawson was a fine student and a promising young man. I know he was dear to many of you, and he will be sorely missed. It's important during times of tragedy to come together for support. Tomorrow, we'll be bringing in a grief counselor to speak with you collectively and individually if you feel you'd like to speak with her. Your parents have also been informed. Right now, I'd like to hand the stage over to some of Brett's teachers, who would like the share their feelings and memories of this fine young man."

The rest of the assembly was a blur. Jaxon sat, miserable and alone, as the golf coach tearfully related some anecdotes about Brett. Then a couple more teachers spoke.

Grief welled up in her, followed by an empty desolation. Jaxon had never before experienced the death of someone she cared about. She had always been alone, with no family or close friends. The system had shuffled her around so much that she didn't have time to get close to anyone, and she never stuck around long enough to see someone pass away.

She didn't know what to do with her feelings, how to handle them, and a terrible, crushing helplessness overcame her. Clawing up from the miserable darkness of her feelings came another emotion, far more vicious and hurtful.

Guilt.

He didn't want to go last night, it whispered in her mind. You made him. *You pestered him until he said yes. Even as you were driving in front of the strip mall, he said he didn't want to go down that alley. It's like he foresaw it, remember? He said he had a bad feeling about going out that night. But you made him.*

It's your fault.

Jaxon cringed. As the teachers went on telling anecdotes about her friend, each mention of Brett's name made her curl up a little more, made her feel a little more responsible.

At last, the teachers let them go. Everyone remained silent as they walked out of the assembly. Jaxon had known Brett was popular, but she hadn't realized just how many people cared about him. Even Courtney looked as if she'd been punched in the gut.

Jaxon noticed that no one went up to offer information to Ms. Dennison or any

of the other teachers. Only Jaxon knew what had happened, why Brett would be in a neighborhood like that in the middle of the night.

But what could she say? Should she tell them? Would that do any good? Jaxon couldn't collect her thoughts. Everything seemed jumbled.

In her car in the parking lot, Isadore was waiting to pick Jaxon up. As she slumped into the seat beside her foster mother, she gave Jaxon one of those stiff hugs that showed she wanted to demonstrate affection she couldn't quite feel.

"Oh, Jaxon, they sent us a text. I'm so sorry! He was a friend of yours, wasn't he?"

Jaxon nodded, not trusting herself to speak. She didn't want to burst into tears in front of the cold, distant woman.

"They say he was murdered. How terrible! But why was he in a bad part of town so late at night?"

Jaxon shook her head, pretending she didn't know.

"Did he tell you anything about that?"

Jaxon shook her head again, feeling as though her denial was a betrayal.

"I'll take you home. You just try to rest and take your mind off it."

Jaxon resisted the urge to smack her. Take her mind off it? A friend of hers, the only one she had in the city, had just been murdered by some teenage thugs, and she was supposed to take her mind off it?

Oh, and Isadore was taking her "home," as if she'd ever had one of those. Jaxon slumped in her seat and stared out the window without seeing anything.

It's my fault. That's all she could think. *It's my fault.*

When they got back to the Grants' mansion, Jaxon begged to use the computer, and to her surprise, her foster parents said yes. They seemed to be Luddites even though Stephen was a scientist and they lived in the middle of America's biggest city. Usually, they only let her use one of the laptops when she did her homework, but they weren't putting up a fuss. Perhaps they felt intimidated by the first real emotions she'd allowed herself to show in front of them.

Jaxon searched through the *LA Times* website, cursing herself as her dyslexia kept making her enter typos the search engine couldn't decipher. Her spelling always came out worse when she felt stressed.

How can you type Brett's name wrong, you idiot!

Finally, she got it right and found a short article on page twenty-five of the morning edition.

A flower show in Beverly Hills got a two-page spread on pages twenty-three and twenty-four.

Seventeen-year-old high-school student Brett Lawson was found murdered in the early hours of this morning on West 79th Street in the Vermont Knolls neighborhood of South Los Angeles.

Police on a routine patrol spotted the body of the Hidden Hills Academy student lying in a garbage dumpster behind a fast-food restaurant. The body lay half inside the dumpster but still clearly visible from the nearby street.

The cause of death was numerous stab wounds to the neck and torso. Abrasions on the victim's knuckles indicate that he put up a struggle. The city coroner puts the time of death at approximately 1:30 a.m.

The victim was not a resident of the neighborhood and had no drugs on his person or in his system, making police question why he was in the area. A wallet containing money and a credit card was still on his person. His vehicle was found parked several blocks away and untouched.

Police have no suspects and are urgently requesting any witnesses to come forward.

Jaxon sobbed and put her face in her hands. A garbage can. Those bastards had stuffed him into a garbage can.

She spent the rest of the day in a miserable haze. Her foster parents wisely left her alone. They canceled her private lessons and did not ask for the computer back. A couple of times, she checked the Internet for more about Brett but found no new information.

The next few days at school felt like a bad dream. Everyone left her alone. Even Courtney looked stricken by the news and forgot to bully her. The grief counselors visited the school, said some nonsense about everyone needing to come together to share their pain and sense of loss, and then went back to their happy lives. Some well-intentioned teacher who knew Jaxon and Brett had been hanging out tried to talk her into seeing the school counselor, but Jaxon brushed him off. Nothing anyone could say could make her pain go away.

In the afternoons, she went through her homework on automatic then had her private lessons. Her yoga instructor never said a word about Brett although she must have known because she went through more relaxation exercises than usual. Jaxon appreciated the sentiment even though the exercises didn't help.

Marquis, her aikido teacher, helped a lot more.

In the afternoons, Jaxon helped Isadore clear out the furniture in one of the rooms in the Grants' mansion and lay down padding on the floor. Marquis would come in his van and unload various weights, exercise equipment, a punching bag, and racks of strange Chinese martial-arts weapons. Marquis hadn't trained her in the weapons yet, but they made an appropriate backdrop. The punching bag was getting a lot of use, though.

Ever since her first lesson, she'd been imagining hitting Courtney when she practiced her punches. She wondered if Marquis would let her paint the brat's face on it but decided asking would be a bad idea. Marquis told Isadore everything that happened in those lessons, and Jaxon's CPS records had already labeled her as a "problem case" with "violent tendencies."

So instead she kept her mouth shut and went through the moves Marquis taught her. Those moves got more interesting every day. At first, he had been teaching her simple blocks and flips, things to keep an attacker from hurting you. Now, he moved on to more aggressive techniques—punches, arm locks, and roundhouse kicks. Jaxon found it a bit strange. Aikido was supposed to be a soft, defensive martial art of deflecting an attacker's force away and stopping them without hurting them, but the more recent techniques were more like combat training. She wondered if her teacher had switched her from aikido to something like kung fu without telling her.

Jaxon didn't care. She thrilled at the idea of punching and kicking her opponents. She kept having to remind herself to pull back on her strength, though. Despite being short and light, she was stronger than a grown man who lifted weights. When one day Marquis put on a pair of padded gloves and had her practice throwing punches at them while he ducked and wove, trying to avoid her, she could see the sweat breaking out on his brow. He backed off step by step, not just to keep her guessing where to land the next punch, but to soften some of the force of her blows. Some of the tougher hits made him hiss through gritted teeth.

That just encouraged her. Rage welled up inside her heart, and a red haze descended over her vision. She imagined she wasn't striking at her martial-arts teacher but at those nasty boys, smashing their leering faces as they surrounded the girl. She fantasized about finding Brett before they descended on him and busting their heads. In her vision, they would get what they deserved, and Brett would still be alive.

Jaxon growled, a deep, inhuman sound of animalistic fury, and threw another punch.

Marquis let out a grunt and stumbled back, turning almost three hundred sixty degrees from the force of the blow. For a moment, he was helpless. Jaxon stepped in for the kill.

For the kill? Jaxon pulled back at the last moment, her fist still poised midair, ready to crack her instructor in the side of the head.

Marquis reacted an instant later, taking a step back and getting into a defensive position, eyes wide with shock.

He's not the enemy, calm down. Get a grip on yourself!

Jaxon forced her arms to go slack, taking several deep breaths to try to slow her racing heart and clear the red haze from her vision.

But the rage remained, bubbling just beneath the surface.

The sound of applause made them both turn. Isadore stood in the doorway, clapping her hands.

"Well done, Jaxon, well done! You're progressing very well."

"I got a bit carried away." Jaxon's voice came out harsh, deep. She barely recognized it as her own.

"Not at all," Marquis said. "You're just finding your pace."

Jaxon suddenly felt embarrassed. Looking down at her feet, she said, "Everyone says I need to control my anger."

"You do," Isadore said. "And that's what you're doing in these lessons. Learning to control your anger, to focus it into something useful."

Jaxon looked at her, puzzled. It seemed so strange that the rich career woman with no children of her own would want to take her in. Isadore and Stephen lived almost like recluses. They never had friends over, only went out for work and shopping, and never talked about anything other than their work and her education. Why would they want to take in a CPS problem case and train her up with all these classes?

"Useful for what?" Jaxon asked.

"Fighting for what's important," Marquis said.

Jaxon looked at him, and their eyes met. She saw determination in those eyes and a bit of fanaticism, and she had a strange inkling that this life was all some sort of illusion. She'd had plenty of adults lie to her over the years and had gotten good at detecting when someone was handing her a line. She wasn't some charity case who had lucked out by getting adopted by millionaires. Maybe that had been the situation at first, but they knew at least some of her potential. No matter how much she'd tried to hide her abilities, Marquis and Isadore had seen she was far stronger and faster than an ordinary girl. They wanted to build that up, to make her into something special.

But what? And why?

"Fighting for what's important." Maybe. She sensed that was the only answer she'd get.

She imagined those boys again, all the other criminals she'd beaten up, all those bullies and pervy foster fathers, and all the evil in the world. Everyone had always dismissed her as useless, but she had found a use for herself.

She thought of Brett, but she didn't feel sad—only angry.

Yes, it had been her fault he had died. Her mistake hadn't been going out in the first place, though, it had been going out unprepared. Their little night adventures were too dangerous for them. She and Brett hadn't really understood the consequences of their actions. They'd been two kids playing with fire, and he got burned.

Next time, she'd be ready.

All those thoughts flashed through her mind in an instant, more felt than spelled out.

She gestured toward the rack of weapons. "Are those just for decoration?"

A smile tugged at the corner of Marquis's mouth.

"For the time being. You need to work on a few things before we start sparring with weapons."

"So you are going to teach me how to use them."

"Later."

"How about now?"

Marquis shook his head.

"You need to learn control first."

"Teach me control, then."

Marquis gestured toward the punching bag hanging from a chain attached to a steel ring in the ceiling.

"First, I think you need to let off a little steam."

Her instructor went to the punching bag, a thick, padded cylinder as big as she was and twice as heavy, and held it steady with both hands. Jaxon got on the opposite side. Isadore stayed at the doorway, watching.

"Straight punches," Marquis told her. "As fast and as hard as you can."

Marquis put one leg behind the other to brace himself.

Jaxon smacked the punching bag with her right fist. It made a satisfying thump against the padding, and Jaxon felt Marquis give a little. She followed with her left, then her right again, picking up speed.

The rage came back, and everything turned red again. Her fists became a blur, the thumps on the punching bag like some techno beat. She had to step forward as Marquis was slowly pushed back inch by inch by the force of her blows.

She picked up the pace. Marquis leaned his entire weight against the bag, both feet braced, his face red and sweaty with strain. Jaxon gave a final punch and heard a loud tearing sound.

She blinked and looked at her hand. She'd broken through the bag, her fist buried in the padding.

Marquis peered around the bag and looked at her arm with wonder.

Isadore let out a low chuckle from her vantage point at the doorway.

"You can add that to your bill, Marquis."

Jaxon yanked her hand out of the hole she had made and found her skin raw. Blood seeped out of little cuts on her knuckles.

My muscles may be strong, but my flesh is like a normal person's. Better remember that.

Marquis bandaged up her hands, and for the rest of the day, he taught her kicks. They used a mannequin on which he had painted red dots that corresponded to all the pressure points in the human body, and he taught her which ones would do the most damage to an opponent. Once again, Jaxon had a feeling he was teaching her something other than aikido.

For several days, it went on like that, each lesson increasingly challenging and increasingly aggressive. But the lessons didn't let her blow off steam. Afterward, the rage seethed inside her. The urge to sneak out at night felt almost overpowering. She wanted to hunt those punks down.

Three things held her back.

First, the neighborhood where they'd fought was miles away, and she didn't have a ride.

Second, she knew they wouldn't be there anyway, not after killing someone. They'd have gone off to have their jollies somewhere else.

Third, Jaxon knew that if she found those kids again, she'd kill them.

In her more rational moments, that thought scared her. Her rage scared her. She'd always been angry—at her parents for ditching her when she was a newborn, at all her crappy foster parents, at her social workers who never understood, and at all the bullies at all the group homes and schools she'd ever been to.

Now, she was enraged at a group of rich kids who wanted to attack a girl and killed a guy just for being a decent human being. At times, that rage overwhelmed her and she caught herself clenching her fists and fantasizing about doing horrible things to everyone who had ever hurt her.

Jaxon felt as if she had been born on another planet. All the cruelty and callousness she saw seemed so alien to her. She'd never act like that, and it scared her to think that people like that might pull her down to their level. She'd started getting too much of a kick out of punishing the bad guys, had started needing it. It had become a bit like addiction, and that addiction had taken away someone she cared about.

Thus, she didn't go out at night hunting for prey. Instead, she hid in Stephen's greenhouse and worked on her part of the garden.

Her foster father was some sort of expert on poisonous plants. He had a big lab at UCLA and did extra work in his own spacious greenhouse in the backyard. Stephen had set aside one corner for her, and that was where she could witness yet another of her strange powers. The inhuman strength and speed were weird enough, but this "talent" was downright inhuman. All she had to do was touch a plant, and it would grow before her eyes. If she held a seed in her hand, it would sprout within seconds.

She'd tested this power when she was living in the Welcome Forever Group Home, exploring its limits. Jaxon found that if she did it for too long, she'd feel fatigued, as if she'd just had an hour-long session with Marquis. The plants seemed to be getting their energy and nutrients from her. The soil around them wouldn't suddenly become dry and barren. A plant took a lot of energy to grow to full size, and she figured doing it so quickly would suck up all the water and nutrients the soil had to offer. Plus, when she made a seed sprout, all she had to do was hold it in her hand. She'd asked Stephen a few sly questions about plant growth and learned that a seed contained its own energy to sprout, so as an experiment she held a seed for longer. She watched in awe as the seed cracked open and let out a little bud before growing milli-meter by millimeter. She shuddered as thin roots coiled around her hand like tentacles while the plant grew to full maturity. There was no way a seed could do all that with its own energy.

Within less than five minutes, she held a perfectly grown daffodil in her hand while she leaned against the wall, panting and exhausted. Her swollen tongue stuck to the top of her parched mouth. After tearing the plant off her hand, she rushed to the sink and gulped down three glasses of water in quick succession. She knew she acted as the soil, somehow transferring from her own resources everything a plant needed—nutrients and water.

The power both enchanted and repelled her. She wanted to come to the greenhouse to relax, not to freak herself out. Her power could be dangerous, too. If she went too far, she knew she might kill herself from dehydration or malnutrition. Therefore, she wore two pairs of gloves to shield the plants from her touch and tended her garden like a normal human being. Then everything felt serene.

Taking care of delicate shoots that would one day turn into vegetables and flowers calmed her, pushing her rage to one side for a little while—at least for as long as she stayed in the greenhouse.

Sometimes, she felt as though she never wanted to leave. The world outside was too ugly.

Every morning and every evening, she asked Stephen and Isadore to lend her one of the laptops so she could check the news. Despite being so picky about technology, they gave her what she wanted without a word. She could find nothing about Brett in the newspaper. Someone had put up a memorial page on Facebook, and a couple of kids at her school shared Instagram photos of him, but otherwise it was like he didn't exist. None of the newspapers, magazines, or popular city blogs mentioned a thing about the murder after that one little story. The police hadn't found the suspects, apparently, and murders happened every day in Los Angeles, so the press had gone on to cover other crimes, other victims.

Brett had become just another statistic.

Chapter 5

July 17, 2016, LOS ANGELES, CALIFORNIA

10:30 A.M.

By the second week after Brett's death, Jaxon had recovered somewhat. The pain had ebbed to a low, background ache. She could function. With a terrible realization, Jaxon knew that things would eventually go back to normal. She would move on with her life, and Brett, while still mourned, would fade into the background. Their conversations would fade. She'd have to think for a moment to remember the punch lines to some of his jokes. By the time she was an old woman, she'd have probably forgotten the make of the car he had been so proud of, maybe even the color of his eyes. To think that everyone would be so forgotten in time, including her, was deeply disturbing. She felt as though she needed to do something with her useless life, to make a mark in the world. She didn't want to be forgotten.

Once the weekend came, Jaxon asked for some pocket money, her phone, and a lift to the nearest bus stop. She wanted some time to herself and planned to wander around Chinatown. Stephen and Isadore, ever the overprotective foster parents, hesitated. Jaxon put on a face, feeling a twinge of guilt at playing the grief card, but she really needed some space. They relented.

An hour later, she strolled through the ornate red lacquered gate of LA's Chinatown. The street was packed with people, only about half of them Chinese. The rest were tourists who gawped at the red paper lanterns hanging from wires strung over the street and at the colorfully painted storefronts topped with sweeping roofs made to look like pagodas. The smell of fried rice and roast duck wafted through the air.

Most of the signs were in both English and Chinese. As she stared at them and the brilliantly painted Asian façades, Jaxon wound her way through a crowd thick with Anglos taking selfies and making Bruce Lee jokes. Jaxon shook her head. She got the brunt of lots of black jokes, mixed-race jokes, and "just what the hell are you, anyway" jokes. At least she didn't get Asian jokes. Her eyes slanted a bit in what was called the epicanthic fold, but most people didn't see enough beyond her skin color to notice. Some middle-aged idiot was pulling the sides of his eyelids and talking like Fu Manchu while his laughing wife filmed him on her cell phone.

Suddenly, a wave of grief washed over her. She leaned against a wall, breathing heavily. Here she was sightseeing while Brett lay dead in the morgue!

But you're not sightseeing, a little voice whispered inside her. *You know why you're here.*

She shook her head to clear it.

Straightening her spine and taking a deep breath, she continued on her way, glancing to her left and right to check out the scene. The main pedestrian thoroughfare was a total tourist trap, with lots of cheap clothing stores and restaurants. As she penetrated further into the neighborhood, though, the number of Anglos reduced, and she saw more and more signs only in Chinese.

She paused at an Asian beauty salon. The window displayed photos of willowy Chinese models with perfect hair and makeup. Peering between them to look inside, she saw a row of little tables where Chinese women worked on the hair and nails of mostly Asian customers. She wondered how they would handle her hair and skin tone. She'd been told by more than one beautician that they didn't know what to do with "black hair." Strange that because she was mixed, people always saw the black before anything else.

Jaxon shrugged her shoulders and moved on from the salon. That wasn't what she'd come for anyway.

As she turned, she caught a glimpse of some guy in a hooded sweatshirt ducking out of sight behind a group of tourists.

Jaxon paused. Had he been looking at her? She scanned the crowd, but too many people were blocking her view, and she lost track of him.

Don't be paranoid. This isn't some trashy neighborhood in the middle of the night. He was probably just checking you out.

Or not. Only Brett and Otto found you attractive.

Wincing with inner pain, she kept walking.

Half a block farther on, she stopped again. In the center of a little plaza next to the main street stood a big fountain sculpted to look like a mountain stream, complete with moss-covered stones. The water sparkled in the bright Californian sun and shone off several little golden statues of Buddha and other Asian figures she assumed were gods and goddesses. Scattered here and there in the water sat little half-submerged brass bowls. Each had a red plastic sign next to it with a phrase like "Happiness," "Long Life," or "Vacation." Coins glinted within the bowls and in the water around them.

Jaxon smiled bitterly. A Chinese wishing well. She could've thought of a thousand wishes.

Beyond the fountain, set back from the street, stood an ornate building that could only be a temple of some sort. It lay open in the front, its interior half hidden by rows of red-and-gold columns and a haze of incense smoke. A giant golden Buddha statue sat, smiling and fat, against the back wall.

Only Chinese people seemed to be going into the temple, so she decided not to enter. She might be part Asian, but she didn't really know and didn't want to intrude on someone else's religious space. The wishing well, though, had signs in English as well as Chinese, so she figured standing there was okay.

She pulled a quarter out of her pocket, aimed for the bowl labeled "Happiness," and tossed the coin.

It splashed dead center into the bowl, but she had thrown it too hard, and the coin bounced out again, landing on the edge of the bowl.

She watched for a moment, waiting to see if the flow of water would push it into the bowl or knock it out, but the coin just rested there, unmoving.

Snorting with disgust, Jaxon turned and continued walking.

A flicker of movement at the edge of her vision caught her eye. He was there again, the guy in the sweatshirt, walking with his hood over his head even though it was ninety degrees. Was he really stalking her?

Nonsense. He was just going with the flow of the crowd, but she could have sworn he had been looking at her and glanced away when she turned.

She picked up her pace and wove through the crowd. After a couple of blocks, she didn't see him anymore. Whether or not he'd really been following her, he was gone. The perv could go ogle some other girl.

The crowd was getting on Jaxon's nerves. It was noisy and annoying, and she realized she wouldn't find what she wanted on a main street anyway. She decided to take a side street that looked less crowded.

As with her walk along Hollywood Boulevard, she was surprised to see how quickly the tourist crowd thinned out and the real neighborhood began. She was one of the only people in sight who wasn't Asian, at least as far as she could tell without knowing her heritage. She could be part Eskimo, as far as she knew. Jaxon saw fewer signs in English, too. The smell of unfamiliar spices wafted out of one restaurant, and next door hung a sign showing a human figure with dots at various points and long explanations in Chinese. She supposed it was an ad for an acupuncturist. Beyond that was a bookstore that she doubted contained anything she could read.

Farther down the street, the gleam of metal blades in a shop window caught her eye.

Bingo.

She strolled over and saw it was a martial-arts store. The sign was only in Chinese, but the display told her all she needed to know. In the window hung a beautiful pair of swords with broad blades and red tassels on the handles. Marquis had taught her enough about martial arts that she knew those tassels weren't just some frilly decoration. Twirling those swords would make the tassels spin in bright circles, distracting the unwary eye for half a second. Sometimes in a fight, half a second meant the difference between winning and losing, and you wouldn't want to lose when faced with those heavy, razor-sharp blades.

Next to them were a pair of nunchucks, and beside those, a variation on the nunchucks that had three sticks instead of just two. Jaxon raised an eyebrow. Those looked tricky to use and seemed even trickier to block. She also spotted a pair of sai, which looked like metal batons about a foot long with two shorter prongs to either side. perfect for catching a blade and yanking it out of the attacker's grasp.

If only Brett had had a pair of those.

She gritted her teeth. It was too late to help Brett, but at least she could help herself.

Stephen and Isadore had given her a hundred bucks, an unusually generous amount for them. She guessed it was pity money or they were trying to buy her affection. She'd had a few foster parents like that.

Whatever. She had enough to buy something here. She'd been sneaking looks at YouTube videos on various martial-arts weapons. With her natural abilities, she could learn on her own. That was why she had come to Chinatown— she wanted to find a good weapon. She had passed a couple of martial-arts stores on the main street, but the stuff all looked cheap and showy.

These weapons looked like the real deal. She'd have to be careful about using it in front of the Grants, but they were pretty clueless anyway. Despite all their weird rules, at least they didn't constantly hover over her like some foster parents did.

She opened the door and stepped into the shop. Chinese music played from some hidden speaker. It sounded strange to her ear, with no beat or rhythm. She never understood the attraction of that type of music, but if one billion people listened to it, she might've missed something.

"May I help you?"

A middle-aged Chinese man with a big bald patch partially hidden by a horrible comb-over stood behind the counter, eyeing her suspiciously. Jaxon tensed. She'd experienced this so many times before. It was called Shopping while Being

Black. She couldn't count the number of times mall security had followed her or some retail snob had hinted that Jaxon should take her business elsewhere. Everyone who actually bothered to look at her could tell she was mixed, but when she entered a store, her skin color was all anyone saw.

"Just browsing." She knew that was the worst thing to say because it made her sound evasive, but she didn't care. Let this guy glare at her all he wanted.

Her gaze passed over a bookshelf filled with books in Chinese, then she found a smaller shelf of books in English. They were all instructional manuals for a bewildering variety of kung fu styles—dragon, snake, mantis, drunken monkey.

Drunken monkey? Some guy had told her about that once, but she thought he had been pulling her leg.

She flipped through the book. Each page had a series of photos of a Chinese man in a field going through various techniques. Apparently, with drunken-monkey kung fu, the fighter stumbled around as though drunk, but those stumbles turned into attacks and blocks. The body twisted and turned in unpredictable ways, making one hard to hit and keeping the opponent guessing about where the next attack would come from. The fighter looked harmless, comical even, but could be deadly.

A bit like me. Jaxon smiled. *I look like a helpless little girl, but I can take a man twice my size. And I don't even have to pretend to be drunk to do it.*

She put the book back and picked up another about a kung fu style called wing chun. She'd heard Marquis mention that it was one of the deadliest martial arts. He'd spent many years learning it under a Chinese master. Out of the corner of her eye, she noticed the shop owner leaning on the counter, staring at her. She ignored him.

The back cover explained that wing chun is an aggressive style that focuses on close-quarter combat. It mixes straight-line punches and kicks with quick, deflective arcs to push away an opponent's attacks. There none of the soft, sweeping moves of aikido in that style of fighting. Jaxon's eyebrows went up when she read that wing chun had been invented by a Buddhist nun named Ng Mui.

"You go, sister." Jaxon chuckled.

The back cover went on to say that it was the favorite style of Bruce Lee.

"I'm sold."

She opened the book. Like the one on the drunken-monkey style, most pages had photos demonstrating the techniques. She flipped through the first few chapters, studying the beginner's moves one by one, and felt a growing sense of confusion that quickly turned into amazement.

That was the technique Marquis had been teaching her! He'd changed styles on her and hadn't even mentioned it.

Jaxon's brow furrowed. Why would he do that?

Wait, what had he said? Something about fighting for what was important.

Marquis was up to something, and her foster parents were in on it. No way of telling what their plans were, though.

She put the book back. She wouldn't need that one.

Turning to the weapons, she looked them over again. She went over to the pair of sai and picked them up. The handles fit her grip as though they were made for it, and the balance felt perfect, like extensions of her arms.

"Don't touch the weapons unless you're going to buy!" the guy behind the counter said.

"I am going to buy something." Jaxon glared back at him.

He gave a derisive chuckle. "You're studying martial arts, little girl?"

Great, he's gone from racism to sexism.

"Yeah, I used to study aikido, but now I'm doing wing chun. What do you study, drunken monkey?"

He gave her a look as though he had just sucked on a lemon. "Ha ha. Very funny."

She turned her back on him and faced the window display again. Just as she did, she saw that guy with the gray hoodie duck out of sight.

Her skin prickled with fear. She'd been right. Someone really was following her.

Her fear faded, replaced with a steely calm.

Fine. Bring it on.

Squaring her shoulders and clenching her fists, she stepped outside.

Chapter 6

July 10, 2016, LOS ANGELES,
CALIFORNIA

11:00 A.M.

Okay, don't screw this up.

Otto shouldered through the Chinatown crowd, keeping his eye on the familiar figure in front of him. Jaxon walked just twenty yards ahead. If he called out her name, she would turn. If he ran up to her, she would be in his arms in just a few seconds.

Instead, he kept his distance even though every nerve in his body urged him to rush forward. It was time to make contact and get Jaxon out of the danger she was in, but Atlantis Allegiance had been ambushed too many times for him to just go blundering up to her like some lovesick puppy.

This could be a trap.

He kept his features hidden under a gray hoodie even though the sun baked down on him.

"See anything?" Otto whispered into the headset.

"Nothing yet, honey," Vivian's sultry voice whispered into his ear. He felt a tingling in his spine at how close it sounded, as though she were right up against him. He could practically feel her breath on his neck, which made him feel unfaithful to the girlfriend he was trying to save.

"Is Grunt in position?" he whispered back.

"No, I'm eating an egg roll five blocks away. What do you think?" the mercenary grumbled in his ear.

That got him out of the mood quickly enough.

Otto was talking into what looked like a hands-free cell phone, but Edward was far too paranoid for anything like that. Instead, the hacker had supplied him with a radio transceiver with a scrambled signal on a frequency sandwiched between two of the radio bands used by the patrol cars of the Los Angeles Police Department.

Otto had laughed when Edward had told him that. "I gotta hand it to you—you got guts!"

Edward had shaken his head. "Guts? Not in this lifetime. Too many dangers—too many hidden conspiracies. I put the frequency there because no one would suspect it. It's not like anyone is going to monitor the police band except the LAPD, and their radios are tuned to set channel frequencies that can't be changed unless you tinker with the radio itself. The cops won't hear anything, and no one else is going to eavesdrop. It's hiding in plain sight."

Otto smiled as he followed Jaxon. That guy might have been a mess, but he knew what he was doing. Even if someone did pick up the frequency, it was scrambled with a military-grade cipher, and only their headsets had the key.

Jaxon had turned a couple of times, and once, Otto could've sworn she'd spotted him, but she kept on going, strolling through the shopping area and casually looking at the displays in the windows.

Keep calm. If she thought you were stalking her, she would have bolted. If she had recognized you, she would have come over. She doesn't suspect a thing. As long as she stays casual, everything's fine. Once Grunt and Vivian check the coast is clear, you can make contact.

Jaxon pushed out of the crowd and went down a side street. Otto slowed, seeing the crowd was much thinner there. He let Jaxon gain some distance on him.

Once he entered the street, he spotted her about half a block away, looking into the window of a shop. She opened the door and entered.

Otto stepped into the street and hurried to catch up.

"We ready yet?" he whispered into his mic.

"Coast is clear from this vantage point, Pyro," Grunt's voice came into his ear.

"Vivian, what about from where you are?"

Silence.

"Vivian? Are we a go?" Otto asked again.

He had made it to the shop's window. Otto cocked his head to see it was a martial-arts shop. Since when had she been interested in that? Otto remembered how she had liked to smack the punching bag at the gym in their group home. She'd been a natural. Was she taking martial arts classes now?

They'd only been separated for a couple of months, but it felt like ages. He'd lived a whole life since then. Apparently, she had too.

Peering through the window, he could make out Jaxon standing in one of the aisles.

He glanced both ways. No one looked suspicious in this street. Why wasn't Vivian giving the go ahead? He waited a full minute, growing more tense by the second.

"Vivian, do you see anything suspicious?"

Jaxon turned towards the window. Otto ducked out of view.

"She ain't responding, Pyro," Grunt said. "I don't know what's wrong."

"Equipment failure?" Otto asked.

"Nope," Edward said over the line. "System all checks out."

Grunt cursed. "I'll go check on her. Don't make contact, Pyro."

Otto took a couple of steps away from the store.

The door opened, and Jaxon stepped out.

Otto's breath caught as she looked right at him.

She stared, incredulous, then her eyes widened in delight. "Otto!"

Jaxon flew into her arms. Otto held her tightly, breathing in her scent. Damn, he'd forgotten how nice she smelled and how good it felt to hold her.

She pulled back to look up at him, her arms still around his middle.

"What are you doing here?" she asked. "Did they let you out of jail?"

"No, they busted me out."

"Busted you out? Who?"

"The Atlantis Allegiance. We came for you."

"Who? Why?"

Otto realized he was babbling like a madman.

"Look, there's no time to explain now, but you're in danger. Remember those guys in the greenhouse? They're still after you. In fact, they've already got you. Come with me."

Grunt's voice came into his ear. "Damn it, Pyro, have you already made contact?"

Otto remembered the mic was open. Everyone could hear everyone else at all times.

"She spotted me. Where's Vivian?"

"Can't find her. Stay put at your present location. I'm coming."

"What's going on?" Jaxon asked as she peered curiously at the headset, half hidden by his hooded sweatshirt.

"If I knew that, I'd tell you. Trouble, most likely," Otto said.

Grunt's voice came into his ear again. "Get her off the street and into a shop. Stay out of sight. I know what street you're on. Once I get there, I'll tell you, and you can come out. But get out of sight right now!"

"What's going on?" Jaxon demanded.

Otto realized the look on his face showed her they were in danger. Without a word, he hustled her back inside the martial-arts shop. The man behind the counter frowned at them.

Otto led her to the last of the store's three aisles, well out of sight of the window. Racks of martial-arts uniforms and padding for sparring matches made a thick barrier that blocked the view from the door and window. Otto bent down so his head didn't show over the top. Jaxon was short enough that she didn't need to.

He turned to her and held her by the shoulders. All he wanted to do was kiss her and tell her how much he had missed her, but that wasn't the time. They never had the time, it seemed.

"Okay, look. Those guys who attacked us in the greenhouse wanted to kidnap you. They were government agents."

"Why would government agents want to kidnap me?"

"I'm getting to that," Otto said. He wanted to leave the most incredible bit of information until the last because it was going to be a lot to absorb. "They know you're something special, that you're stronger and quicker than the average person."

Jaxon's eyes widened. "How did you know that?"

"I kinda sensed it in the gym, but you're not the only one like that. There's a whole bunch of you. You all have special powers. Not just strength and speed but stuff that's almost magical. A scientist who studies you guys told me all about it. The government wants you for some reason. When they couldn't kidnap you, they tried a more subtle way."

Jaxon studied him, and realization slowly dawned on her face. "They adopted me?"

Otto nodded. Cute and strong, and she turned out to be a pretty quick thinker.

Jaxon's jaw dropped. After a moment, she spoke. "It makes sense now. Stephen and Isadore never seemed the type to adopt, and they got me this martial-arts teacher who's been training me to become some sort of fighter."

"What are you doing back here?"

Jaxon and Otto turned. The proprietor stood at the end of the aisle, a frown on his face and his hands on his hips.

"Sorry, sir," Otto said. "I just needed to talk to my girlfriend."

Jaxon squeezed his hand. Otto smiled at her. That made all the craziness of the past couple of months worth it.

The proprietor gestured angrily toward the door. "Go have your little love chat somewhere else. I have a business to run."

Otto couldn't help but notice no other customers in the store. With that guy's attitude, Otto wasn't surprised.

"What's going on out there?" Edward asked.

"We're waiting for Grunt," Otto said into his handless mic.

The shopkeeper looked at him like he was a lunatic. Otto waved the wire to show he wasn't talking to himself. He got a scowl in return.

"Well, where the hell is he?" Edward asked.

"Hold on," Grunt whispered.

"What?" Otto said.

"Hold on," Grunt said, his voice barely audible.

The Chinese guy took a step closer. "Look, I've had enough of this."

Otto waved him away. He turned to Jaxon, about to tell her to stay out of sight of the window, when his earpiece erupted with what sounded like gunshots. The proprietor jerked his head towards the entrance, as did Jaxon. Otto pulled the earpiece out and could still hear the shots, cracking one after another in rapid succession in the distance.

"Please tell me that's fireworks." Jaxon's face paled.

"Chinese New Year is months away," the storeowner said. "Sounds like a robbery or a gang fight. You kids better stay here until the police take care of it."

Jaxon and Otto both nodded. The guy went up a peg in Otto's estimation.

Otto stuck the earpiece back in his ear.

"What's going on out there?" he demanded.

More shots. The sound of running feet.

Then Grunt's voice ripped into his eardrum. "Incoming!"

Otto grabbed Jaxon and the storekeeper and threw them down onto the floor along with himself.

The Chinese guy slapped his hands away. "Are you crazy? What's the matter with you?"

"Stay down!"

The man tried to stand up, and Otto pulled him down again.

"Kid, if you don't let go, I'll—"

He cut off midsentence as the door creaked open.

Silence.

The storeowner looked at Otto, pointed toward the door, hidden from view behind the rack of clothing, and mouthed the words, "Who is that?"

Otto shrugged. He didn't know. All he knew was that it was someone he really, really didn't want to meet.

Footsteps.

Someone walked down the farthest aisle of the store then turned and walked down the next. Whoever it was walked slowly, deliberately, without pausing but without any hurry.

The footsteps passed on the other side of the rack of martial-arts uniforms. Otto caught a vague glimpse of a figure through a gap in the clothing. He eased his Taser out of his pocket. The storeowner choked back a gasp when he saw it but was smart enough not to say anything. A few more shots rang out in the distance, along with some faint screams.

A woman stepped around the end of the aisle and glared at them. Otto recognized her from a photo Edward had shown him—Isadore Grant, General Meade's top assassin.

Otto aimed the Taser and fired.

With impossible speed, Isadore ducked to one side, and the twin darts implanted themselves in the back wall. Isadore took three long strides and leapt toward Otto, one foot extended in a kick. He brought up his hands to protect his face, knowing that would only mean postponing his death for a few seconds.

With a blur of motion, Jaxon blocked the kick, making Isadore pirouette in midair.

The assassin landed nimbly on her feet, facing Jaxon. The two stood there for a moment, glaring at each other from only a few inches away.

"What's going on?" Jaxon demanded.

"These are criminals," Isadore said. "They've come to kidnap you."

"She's lying," Otto cut in. "She's a government assassin. They hired her to be your foster mother and train you to do their dirty work for them!"

Isadore dismissed his words with an impatient gesture. "That's ridiculous. A government conspiracy over a sixteen-year-old girl? Don't be stupid."

"A sixteen-year-old girl with superhuman powers," Otto said. "No way a normal kid could be as strong and as fast as she is. She's probably got other powers too, don't you Jaxon?"

Jaxon turned and looked at him in amazement. "Why yes, I..." She let her sentence trail off and turned to her foster mother. "You'd have to tell me sooner or later, so what gives?"

Isadore paused for a moment, assessing Jaxon. Finally, she nodded.

"Yes, you are a special girl. We knew about your strength and speed. That's why we hired Marquis. And we knew you needed to learn how to control it, hence the yoga lessons. But there's more to it than that. You're far more powerful than we ever imagined. What you can do with plants is incredible."

Jaxon's breath caught. Isadore went on as the crackle of gunfire continued in the background.

"Your potential was wasted in the CPS system. You'd have ended up as a criminal or a suicide case. Many of your kind do. They don't know how to adjust to normal human society. We're offering you a home, Jaxon—a chance to live up to your potential. You can rise high, have a good career, wealth, respect, a family."

Jaxon hesitated, and her features softened for a moment then grew stony. "Who hired you?"

Otto cut in. "General Meade. He's part of a secret plan to collect people like you"—he almost said "Atlanteans" but decided against it since Jaxon was being asked to take in so much already—"and he's making his own private army. This isn't a government project. This is a government within the government, and they plan to overthrow democracy and rule for themselves."

"Foolish boy." Isadore sneered. "You have no idea what you're involved in. You don't know the dangers facing our planet."

Our planet? That seemed like an odd choice of words.

Jaxon and Otto slowly backed away. The storeowner had disappeared.

"I think the real danger I'm facing is right in front of me," Jaxon whispered. "You lied to me. Lied to me about everything."

"It was necessary," Isadore said, taking a step forward. "Come with me, and your friend won't get hurt. He's an escaped convict, you know."

"He's innocent," Jaxon said, still backing away.

They rounded the end of the aisle. Isadore followed, legs slightly bent, body half turned in a fighting stance. She reminded Otto of a stalking tiger he'd seen on the Discovery Channel once.

"The courts don't think so, and your sheltering him is a felony. You could go to juvenile detention, maybe even be tried as an adult. Instead of having the world in the palm of your hand, you'd be worse off than when I found you."

"I don't trust you," Jaxon said, tears welling in her eyes. "Why does everyone have to lie to me?"

"He's the one lying, Jaxon. He's part of a renegade band of criminals. They want to use you for their crimes. But I'll let him go. We won't even mention he was here at all. Stephen and I only want to make sure you're safe and can develop your potential."

"What's that shooting?" Jaxon asked.

The firefight seemed to be dying down, but the occasional shot still crackled in the distance.

"Otto's gang going on a rampage. The police will get here soon. If you want your friend to stay out of prison, come with me now. I'll let him go and won't say a word to the police. You'll have everything—

wealth, a future, a place to belong—and he'll have his freedom."

Isadore extended a hand.

Jaxon hesitated. She looked from Otto to her foster mother and back again.

"Perhaps you should go, Otto," Jaxon whispered.

"No way, I busted out of jail to save you. She's going to use you as a weapon. She's the criminal!"

Otto gripped Jaxon's shoulders, and together they continued to back away toward the door.

"What have I ever done to hurt you, Jaxon?" Isadore said. "I've opened up my home to you, offered you a good education. We'll pay for college and beyond. Just let your friend walk away, and you'll have a life. That's what you've always wanted, isn't it? There's not much time. The police will be here any minute. If they find him here, he's finished. Come with me, Jaxon."

Jaxon gave Otto a confused look. He shook his head.

"I'm not going anywhere," he said. "I'm not letting you go again."

"Think of your friend, Jaxon. He'll go to jail for years for this."

Jaxon turned back to Otto, her shoulders slumped. Her hand reached for his, and their fingers interlocked. "She's right. There's no use. Go and save yourself, Otto. If I run away with you, they'll just hunt me down."

"No way, I'll—"

The door burst open, slamming against the back wall and snapping off one of its hinges. Grunt stood panting in the doorway as the door hung crazily on the bottom hinge. His jeans were soaked with blood down one side, and his face was pale and sweaty. His eyes fixed on Isadore and went wide.

"You!" Grunt and Isadore said in unison.

Grunt whipped out a pistol from the hidden holster inside his leather jacket. Otto screamed and threw Jaxon to the floor, landing on top of her to shield her from any bullets.

He didn't need to bother. Isadore leapt to the bookshelf, grabbed a heavy volume, and threw it with such force and accuracy that it struck Grunt in the wrist and made the gun fly out of his hand.

"It's time to finish this!" Isadore roared as she ran up the aisle toward him.

"Damn straight!" Grunt yelled back, reaching for the weapons display in the window and grabbing one of the broad Chinese swords. He whipped it out of its metal scabbard, which he threw at her head.

Isadore tucked into a roll, and the scabbard shot right over her to smash a mirror behind the counter. A squawk from beneath the counter told Otto where the shopkeeper had disappeared to.

Isadore rolled to her feet in front of Grunt but still out of reach of his sword. His face red with rage, the mercenary paced toward her.

"This is for Morocco," he snarled.

He made a vicious swing at her head that Isadore dodged easily. He swung again and missed again, the blade slicing through a stack of books, sending papers flying.

Isadore blocked his next swing by grabbing his arm and flipping the huge man over her head to bring down the bookshelf with a crash.

Grunt was back on his feet in an instant, his hand still gripping the sword. He lunged, aiming for Isadore's stomach, but she bent her body, and the blade cut nothing but air. She grabbed his arm again and used her other hand to smack him in the face with her fist. Then, she brought her knee up against his wrist. Grunt bellowed with pain, and the sword clattered to the ground.

Otto looked around, desperate to find a way to help. Jaxon looked just as confused as he was. She must have been going crazy to see a guy who looked like Grunt trying to cut her foster mother in half.

The shopkeeper peeked over the counter.

"Do something!" Otto shouted.

"What, you think all Chinese people are black belts? You racist, I only have this store to put my son through college!"

Shaking his head, Otto looked back at the fight to see Grunt and Isadore rolling on the ground, trading punches. Grunt did not look like he was winning.

Then Otto saw something else—Grunt's pistol lying at the other end of the aisle, right next to the two fighters and not ten feet away from him.

Otto leapt to his feet, ran to the gun, and scooped it up.

He aimed it at the tangle of fists and limbs at his feet. "Hold it right there!"

Grunt grinned up at him, smiling with a split lip that dripped blood. "Hey, Pyro! Looks like you're good for something after all."

Otto gestured at Isadore, trying to keep his hands steady as his entire body trembled. "Get up and move to one side."

"I'm calling the police!"

That was from the shopkeeper, who had stood up and was holding a phone in his hand.

"Don't do that!" everyone shouted at once.

The shopkeeper stared at the brutish mercenary, the kid with a gun, the nondescript woman with the crazy martial-arts moves, and the teenage girl who had run up to the weapons display and grabbed a pair of sai, and he let the phone slip out of his hand to clatter on the floor.

Otto turned back to Isadore. "Okay, we're walking out of here with you in front. If any of General Meade's goon squad is out there, you'll be the first to get it."

Grunt chuckled and walked over to him, taking the gun. "Cut it out, Pyro, you sound like a damn movie. Besides, you couldn't shoot anyone with that thing."

"Yeah, I could," Otto said, feeling defensive.

"No, you couldn't," Grunt replied, flicking a switch on the side of the gun. "You left the safety on."

Otto blushed.

Grunt pointed the gun at Isadore, who glared at them and looked ready to pounce.

"You're just as good as you always were, baby. I barely had time to draw my weapon before you sent it flying across the room."

A slow smile spread across Isadore's lips. "Oh, Bill, you still know how to show a girl a good time. But hitting a lady? Tsk tsk."

"You're no lady," Grunt grumbled.

"You okay, um, Bill?" Otto asked, indicating the soaking-wet bloodstain on his shirt and the blood dripping down his side.

"Just a graze. I'll be fine. And don't call me Bill."

"It isn't his real name anyway," Isadore said. "I never knew his real name."

The distant wail of a police siren made them all freeze. It drew closer.

Otto glared at the shopkeeper, who remained frozen behind the counter.

"It wasn't me!" the man said, his hands over his head. "Just get out of here!"

Grunt jabbed a finger at the terrified shopkeeper and asked Otto, "Is he always like that?"

Otto nodded. "I think so, yes."

The siren grew louder.

"Time to go." Grunt glanced between Otto and Jaxon. "You kids coming?"

Otto looked at his girlfriend. She was staring at the angry, bloodied killer that had been her foster mother.

"Yes," Jaxon said.

"Move it," Grunt ordered. Isadore went through the door first, hands above her head. Grunt came right behind her with the gun leveled at her back.

Just as Jaxon was about to step out, she tucked the sai in her belt, grabbed a pair of nunchucks, and turned to the proprietor. "These weapons come out to eighty bucks. Keep the change." She placed the hundred dollars Stephen and Isadore had given her on the nearest shelf.

Otto took her hand, and they hurried out of the store.

As they emerged, a car screeched to a halt at the end of the abandoned street. Otto leapt with fright, thinking the cops had arrived already, but immediately relaxed as he saw it was a civilian car with Vivian at the wheel.

Otto hustled Jaxon toward the car. Looking back over his shoulder, he saw Grunt get out of reach of Isadore and hide his gun inside his jacket.

"You're making a mistake not killing me, Bill," Isadore shouted after him.

"I don't shoot down people in cold blood."

Isadore smirked. "Not anymore. Be seeing you!"

The assassin turned and ran the opposite direction as the police siren wailed closer.

Chapter 7

July 12, 2016, SOMEWHERE IN THE
ARIZONA DESERT

8:30 P.M.

After the fight in the martial-arts shop,
the pack of weirdos calling themselves
the Atlantis Allegiance drove her through
the back roads of Los Angeles in a convo-
luted pattern to avoid pursuit, changing
cars three times. Each time, the car was
fetched by the strange woman named
Vivian, who managed to look glamorous
despite a fresh black eye, a bullet wound
through her leg, and another bullet hole
through her purse.

"Bit of trouble with the boys, darling. Government agents have no class," she said.

Each car was a different make and model from the previous one, and Jaxon got the impression they were all stolen, not that she got a good look at the vehicles or anything else since Otto told her to keep her head down and stay out of sight because General Meade's agents were everywhere.

Also, that gave her a close-up view as she witnessed her boyfriend treating Grunt's gunshot wound in the blood-soaked backseat.

"No, Pyro, not that way!" said Grunt. "Here, give me the needle. I'll do my own damn stitches."

Then came a rendezvous in the desert with some geeky scientist named Yuhle, who asked, "Can't you guys go anywhere without getting shot at?", an even geekier guy named Edward, who said, "Sorry about your phone, Jaxon. I short-circuited it remotely so no one can trace the GPS. Can't be too careful," and a Japanese-American scientist named Yamazaki who wouldn't stop staring at her and said, "You have no idea how important you are. May I take a blood sample?"

She had gone from a group home to a foster home to a lunatic asylum.

They were camped out in the middle of nowhere in the Arizona desert while Grunt and Vivian cleaned their weapons and Edward locked himself inside a trailer doing God-knows-what with a satellite uplink.

At least she could be with Otto again. They stayed close all day, hiking in the little valleys between the rough hills that hid their camp, admiring the saguaro cacti that stood as tall as trees and watching the sunset turn the ruddy cliffs from gold to crimson. At night, they looked for meteors in the star-filled sky as the Milky Way traced a faint, glimmering arch high overhead.

Jaxon had spent most of her life in cities and had never gotten to experience such natural beauty. To share it with Otto made it doubly special.

They also shared all that had happened to them in the past few weeks. If not for the fight in Chinatown and their crazy getaway through the streets of Los

Angeles, she would have never believed his tale of gun battles, hidden tracking devices, ambushes, and renegade Native Americans.

And she'd thought her life was weird.

Still, Otto trusted his strange friends, and Jaxon got the feeling that she should too. Otto seemed dedicated to the people and was accepted by everyone despite Grunt's constant teasing. Her boyfriend had that same easy way with them that he had with everybody. That was what had attracted her to him back at the group home. She had always been a bit in awe of people like that, as if they had some magic secret that her awkwardness and shyness kept her from discovering.

After a couple of days of rest, Vivian and Grunt looked much better. Jaxon marveled at how they could shrug off gunshot wounds like paper cuts, but the two mercenaries just said they were "flesh wounds" and "nothing important."

The two scientists, Yamazaki and Yuhle, poked and prodded her, taking blood and DNA samples, running a bunch of medical tests, and asking her all sorts of questions about her powers. They put her through various physical tests like lifting large stones and running up and down steep hillsides in the hot sun. Even Grunt was impressed by the results.

"Don't piss off your girlfriend, Pyro. She'll tear you in half."

They also tested her ability to grow plants and confirmed what she'd suspected about how her powers worked. By the end of the second day, the saguaro cacti around their campsite had grown noticeably taller, and she had to constantly chug water to keep from getting dehydrated.

"Careful with that ability," Dr. Yamazaki warned. "If you learn to do it faster and more powerfully, you might hurt yourself."

Then came a series of tests to look for other powers. Yuhle showed her a deck of cards with various symbols on them, like a star or three wavy lines, and then hid them from her, looking at them one by one while she tried to read his mind and tell him which card he had drawn. She blew that test, which actually came as a relief. At least she was a little bit like normal people! Other tests to predict the future or find hidden objects or break up clouds in the sky just by looking at them didn't work either.

"Can people really do this stuff?" Jaxon objected.

"You can make plants grow simply by holding them," Yuhle said with a shrug, "so I think it's time to throw skepticism out the window."

She didn't have an answer for that. The tests continued, searching for any trace of other paranormal powers. They even took her to an old graveyard at the site of a little ghost town, and she had to try to commune with the dead. Luckily, that didn't work out.

For some reason, though, she didn't tell them about being able to move objects without touching them. They tested her for that too, and Jaxon felt immense relief when that power didn't manifest itself. She hadn't been practicing much because it freaked her out. Too much strange stuff was going on in her life already.

After dinner on the third night, the Atlantis Allegiance sat down around a fire at the center of their campsite. Even Edward came, which surprised Jaxon.

He usually hid in his trailer 24/7. Jaxon sensed something was up.

Grunt spoke first. "We can't stay here. Meade's goon squad has proven too damn resourceful. If we've learned one thing from those bastards, we've learned to keep moving. The question is, where to?" He turned to Dr. Yamazaki.

The scientist looked at Jaxon with a worried expression. "Well, that depends on you, Jaxon. We need to find more people like you, more people of your race."

"I'm mixed race," Jaxon said.

Dr. Yamazaki shook her head. "No, you only look mixed race. You're actually a distinct race that's a blend of all the other races or perhaps the original race. You're Atlantean."

"Huh?"

"As in Atlantis," Otto said.

"Yeah, I get it," Jaxon said, "but that makes no sense. Atlantis is a myth."

"We don't think so," Yuhle said, adjusting his glasses. "We've been studying people like you for some time now. Many supposedly mixed-race people carry what we call the Atlantis gene. From what we can tell, it goes back thousands of years to a common source. We think that there really was an Atlantis that sank into the Atlantic Ocean several thousand years ago. You and the other Atlanteans are descendants of the survivors of that disaster."

Jaxon chewed on that for a minute. "So, I'm some sort of alien or something?"

"No, you're human," Yamazaki said. "You just have some extra genes, ones that give you powers. I met some of your people not so long ago. General Meade had given me a drug that induced a stroke in my brain. I was lying in the hospital, almost a vegetable."

The scientist shuddered. Yuhle put a reassuring hand on her shoulder. She took a minute before going on.

"I could barely move. My thoughts were all scrambled. I couldn't even feed myself. Then a group of people who looked just like you snuck into my room. One woman touched my head, and within minutes, all the effects of my stroke had vanished. Most people take years to make even a partial recovery from a serious stroke, and here I am, perfectly fine."

"Where are those people? Can I meet them?" Jaxon asked, leaning forward.

Dr. Yamazaki shook her head sadly. "They were all killed during the escape. And I don't have any contact information for any of the other subjects I studied over the years. General Meade stole all those files."

Jaxon slumped. For a moment, she'd thought she would actually find people like her.

As if reading her thoughts, Dr. Yuhle said, "We know where we can find more Atlanteans—over in Morocco in northwest Africa."

"Why Morocco, and how can you really know Atlantis was real?" Jaxon asked.

"My old professor made that discovery," Dr. Yamazaki said. "He spent his entire career studying the Atlantis legend. Cultures all around the Atlantic have stories of a great civilization that disappeared when the island it was on sank to the bottom of the ocean. The most famous of those stories is the Greek legend that the philosopher Plato wrote about, but it's found in a lot more sources than that. The ancient civilizations of northern and western Africa had traditions about Atlantis, and there seem to have been similar stories among the Native American tribes in the Caribbean. We don't know much about those because most of those tribes got wiped out within a century after Columbus landed."

"So the legends are true?"

The scientist nodded. "The details vary from culture to culture, but the core idea of a lost civilization in the Atlantic Ocean seems to be true. I'm a geneticist, and I study the history of how certain genes spread through populations over time. The Atlantis gene, actually a whole string of genes, seem to have come from a single population several thousand years ago and spread first to northwest Africa, where Morocco is today."

"Check this out," Otto said, handing a tablet over to Jaxon.

Jaxon stared. The screen displayed a photo of a woman in loose robes and a Muslim headscarf. Behind her was a village in the mountains, with simple whitewashed one-story buildings and goats standing in the street.

But it was the woman who captured her attention.

She could have been Jaxon's mother or aunt. She had the same dark skin, the same broad cheekbones, the same Asian eyelids, and the same brilliant blue eyes.

"I punched a bunch of typical Atlantean features into a facial-recognition program," Edward explained. "Then I did a Google image search for matches. Most came up in northern and western Africa and the Caribbean."

"It's not the most scientific method"—Dr. Yamazaki shrugged—"but it supports the genetic data."

Jaxon was only half listening. She scrolled through the photo gallery, seeing face after face that echoed her features, her lost identity. Some were in what looked like Third World cities, others in mountains or along a brilliantly sunny coastline. Many more looked like they lived in the desert.

It took her a while to be able to speak. "These are my people."

The words came out sounding strange. She'd never had a people before. She'd always thought of herself as mixed race, and not knowing her parents meant she couldn't really attach herself to one group or another. But she was of a particular race, a hidden race, one she had dismissed as only a legend.

"Yes, they are your people, and they're a very special people," Dr. Yamazaki said. "My old professor has been digging through everything he could find that has ever been written on Atlantis. There's a lot of junk, of course, but he found some gems too. In the Renaissance, some of the leading European scholars thought that Atlantis had been located right off the western Moroccan coast. Several archaeological sites on that coastline show an early, advanced civilization. When Atlantis sank, the survivors would have made for the nearest shore. Today, Morocco is one of the most mixed countries in the world. There are Arabs; Berbers, who have African features but white skin; Europeans; Jews; and black Africans. All these people mingle, of course, so there's a huge mixed-race population. You wouldn't look out of place there at all, Jaxon. That's why we think most of the Atlanteans decided to hide there."

Jaxon tensed.

"Hide?"

"Throughout history, people have always feared any community that stood apart and had different traditions," Edward said. "Look at how the Jews have been treated over the centuries... or the Gypsies. Did you know that Hitler threw the Gypsies into the concentration camps right alongside the Jews? He wanted to wipe them out too. He killed more than a quarter of a million of them, but there's still so much prejudice against the Gypsies that their Holocaust has been almost forgotten. Imagine what he would have done if he knew about the Atlanteans. He would have killed them all."

"Or used them as weapons," Grunt said.

A chill went down her spine. Yeah, as weapons. That's what Stephen and Isadore wanted to turn her into. They didn't see her as a human being, just a tool.

Otto put a hand on hers. "We want to go find these people. Maybe they've kept some of the old stories. We could learn more about what happened to Atlantis."

Jaxon cocked her head and looked at Dr. Yamazaki. "I wasn't born in Morocco, was I?"

"Probably not," she replied. "Your CPS records show you were a newborn foundling. Chances are you were born right here in the United States. Atlantis sank thousands of years ago, and so the Atlanteans have had a long time to spread across the globe."

Jaxon perked up. "You said you met others like me. Could any of them have been my parents?"

"I don't think so. You were left at the door to a clinic in San Francisco, and I can remember studying only a couple of subjects from there. Neither of them were old enough to be your parents. Sorry, Jaxon."

She sighed and looked back at the photos. "So it looks like if I want to find myself, I have to go to Morocco. Wait, go to Morocco? I've never even left the West Coast. I don't even have a passport!"

"That won't be a problem, honey," Vivian said.

Jaxon rolled her eyes. "Uh oh. This is going to be one of those crazy, illegal plans you people always make that ends up in a gunfight."

Dr. Yuhle shook his head and sighed. "Almost certainly."

Otto laughed and high-fived Grunt. "Welcome to the Atlantis Allegiance!"

Jaxon gave her boyfriend a sidelong glance. He'd changed, and she wasn't sure she liked all the changes.

Vivian smiled. "Don't worry. I have a contact who can get us real, government-approved passports, but they'll have different names on them."

"Then they're not real passports," Jaxon objected.

"They're real enough in the sense that they work, honey, and the government will be none the wiser."

Jaxon rubbed her temples. She was getting a headache.

"We have to go," Otto said. "It's the only way. Please say yes."

The old, bitter anger welled up in Jaxon. They wanted her to go off to a country she could barely point at on a map and probably end up in worse danger than she already faced. Those guys seemed to attract danger as she attracted bullies. But what choice did she have? She couldn't go back to Isadore and Stephen, not after she had learned the truth about them, and she couldn't live on her own. She wouldn't last a week before the cops picked her up and threw her back in the system, and then General Meade and his goons would get her for good. So no, she had to leave everything she knew and fly halfway across the world, and she didn't have any real say about it. Once again, she was being shuffled around like a suitcase.

Then, something made her pause. So what if she left everything behind? She had nothing in her life in California. Her only real friend besides Otto was dead, and she had no future the way things were going. The chance at going to college and having a somewhat normal life and career had disappeared when she ran away from the Grants, and if she struck out on her own, she would be hunted down and end up as a lab rat. Even if she did manage to avoid capture, she would have to constantly move, working menial jobs in hick towns, never being able to stay long enough to put down roots. She would be a broke fugitive all her life. At least if she went with this pack of weirdos, she would be accepted for what she was and might even find out more about the truth of her past.

For once, she was being forced into a decision that was actually good for her. She still didn't like that she had no real freedom to choose.

"I guess I'll go." She sighed.

* * *

Getting the fake passports proved surprisingly easy. Edward had contacted someone he knew via the Darknet, the hidden part of the Internet invisible to search engines. Parts of the Darknet acted as a sort of criminal supermarket, where you could buy anything from guns to drugs to new identities.

After a long drive to a dusty town in west Texas—little more than a few houses, a trailer park, and a gas station—they stopped at a pleasant ranch house owned by Edward's contact.

The passport forger did not look like a criminal. Instead, he looked like some boring, middle-aged businessman who spoke with a trace of a foreign accent Jaxon couldn't place. Each member of the Atlantis Allegiance had a photo taken, and within a few hours, the mysterious man presented them their new passports. Everyone got a fake name and a fake date of birth close enough to their real one that it looked plausible. There were even stamps from foreign countries on them.

Edward handed the forger a thick wad of hundred-dollar bills. Jaxon's eyebrows shot up.

"Where did you get all that money?" she blurted out.

And come to think of it, where does all the money for this whole operation come from?

Edward blushed and stuttered. Immediately, Jaxon felt sorry. He was socially awkward, and she had just caught him off guard with a probing question. Otto answered for him.

"He's got an online job that pays very well."

She rolled her eyes. "Do I even want to know?"

"Y-you do," Edward stuttered before glancing at the man he had just paid. "But... later."

Jaxon looked at her passport, flipping through the pages. She'd become Alison Ward, born May 15, 2000. She'd been to Mexico twice and England once.

"The fake me has had a more interesting life than the real me." She snorted and looked at the forger. "So are you sure these will work?"

"I'm sure. I've used them plenty of times." Grunt held up his own and grinned. "Looks like I have a new name. That makes seventeen so far!"

"I thought you weren't coming with us," Jaxon said.

"He is," Otto said.

Grunt glared at him. "I'm not. But I need to get out of the country for a while. Getting too hot around here."

The forger turned to Jaxon. "You don't need to worry about this passport being detected. It's genuine as far as the government knows. You've been given the identity of someone who died in infancy. I've altered the government databases to add all the information you see on this document. As far as the government's concerned, you are Alison Ward."

He handed her a manila envelope. "This is your other documentation: social-security number, list of previous addresses. I decided to make you and Otto minors. Travel would be easier if your passports said you were over eighteen, but neither of you look it, so this will reduce the chance of any sticky questions. I made you homeschooled because that cuts out any trouble from assigning you to a school you never went to. Too many times in this business, I've seen incautious people trying to start a new life talk and talk about their fake past and get tripped up by someone who's actually been to those places. Vivian is your mother, by the way. Your father was a black man who died fifteen years ago. It's easier if you don't have to make up memories about a real person you never met."

The forger's words unsettled her. How could he speak so casually about robbing the dead of their identities and fooling the government? Jaxon walked out of the room to the front hall, staring at her new passport, her new self. So much had happened in the past few days that she had trouble making sense of it all.

Vivian walked up to her and put an arm around her. Jaxon tensed. She'd never gotten used to people showing her affection. Well, except for Otto, and she wasn't even fully comfortable with him yet.

"Looks like we're family now, huh?" the mercenary said.

Jaxon seethed. *Yeah, fake family. The only kind I've ever had.*

She tried to block her anger. Vivian was only trying to be nice. The mercenary couldn't have understood how many times Jaxon had heard those very same words from people who never ended up giving a damn about her.

Vivian must have felt her tension because she let go but kept close. "Women have to stick together, honey. I'm on your side."

"You're a mercenary. You fight for money."

Vivian's eyes hooded. "You got an attitude on you, that's for sure. But yeah, I'm getting paid. I got bills you don't know about. I can't afford to fight for free. But at least this time, I'm fighting for the right side."

"What do you mean?"

"Grunt and I used to work for General Meade. That was years ago, when you were a little kid and we were young and stupid and obeyed orders without questioning them."

"What did he order you to do?"

Vivian's face darkened. "We got tangled up in the politics in that region we're going to and ended up attacking the wrong side. We thought we were the good guys, but the man giving the orders sure wasn't."

"So is that why Grunt won't be coming with us?"

"He's coming. He's gotten quite attached to Otto, although good luck ever getting him to admit it. In our business, you move around a lot and lose a lot of people along the way. I think Grunt and I are both looking for a bit of stability, and Otto provides that in a strange way. Otto needs someone to look up to like Grunt, and Grunt... Well, he needs someone to look up to him. It grounds him."

"So are we going to be in danger in Morocco?"

"Not from the situation in the country itself. The country is stable, unlike a lot of North Africa. The king has really clamped down on Islamic terrorist groups. And the streets are safe enough, especially if you have us along."

"That's good, but what I'm really asking is if you guys have any enemies over there who might come after us."

Vivian's face darkened. "None who are alive." She paused, looking as though she was going to say something more, but then shook her head. "Never mind. I don't want to talk about this."

You don't want to talk about it, but we're heading back to where it all happened? I think you and Grunt are going to have to face whatever it is sooner or later.

Chapter 8

July 13, 2016, ALBUQUERQUE, NEW
MEXICO

8:45 A.M.

General Meade glared across his desk at two of his best agents. He'd trusted Stephen and Isadore not to screw this up, but they had. Royally.

The first part of their plan had worked perfectly. Faced with danger and death, Jaxon had grown ever more violent. With a bit of guidance and training, the natural anger that had developed throughout her loveless childhood could have been honed razor sharp. With a few months more training, they could have turned her into a killing machine.

But then the Atlantis Allegiance had shown up and ruined everything. Meade guessed he shouldn't blame Stephen and Isadore too much. Stephen wasn't a fighter, and Isadore had faced someone who was almost her match, an old henchman of Meade's, in fact. Isadore's makeup wasn't quite hiding all the bruises.

His blood still boiled, though. He wanted nothing more than to send those two to some warzone in an awful, disease-ridden jungle somewhere. Sometimes, Meade wished he was serving in the Russian army instead. Being able to threaten people with Siberian exile must have been nice.

Meade rang a buzzer on his desk to summon Orion. Stephen and Isadore stared as the Atlantean strode in, his muscles rippling under his bodysuit as he moved with catlike grace.

"This is Orion, our prototype," Meade told them. "I've mentioned him before. We've used drugs to kill his old personality, and now he's little more than a slave."

That last word turned Meade's stomach. He hated to do that to a man—it went against everything he stood for—but larger issues were at stake. He'd rather have one man be a slave than the entire human race.

"Isadore, you and Orion are a team now. Get training and learn to work together. You'll see just how advanced the Atlanteans can be, and he's still at the beginning of his training. Orion is your superior in strength and speed, but he doesn't have your experience. He's like a child. You'll have to direct him as you were directing Jaxon. Unlike her, he'll obey you completely. I've given him that order, and he'll obey even as far as dying for it. Don't expect much initiative from him, though, at least not yet. You'll be training that into him. Once we locate where they've taken Jaxon, we're going to send you in."

"How do you want me to handle this?" she asked.

"In your usual way. Kill them all. They know too much."

"And Jaxon?"

"If you can capture her easily, we'll bring her back and work on her with the drugs we've developed. It would have been better to go the slow way, raise her up and indoctrinate her, but it looks like that's not an option anymore."

"What if I can't capture her easily?"

"Then kill her," Meade snapped, "but bring back her body. It would be interesting to do an autopsy and see if there are any internal difference from regular humans." He turned to Isadore's husband. "Stephen, brew up some of your poisons. Your wife is going on a trip."

"Have you located them already?" Stephen asked.

Meade shook his head. "They've gone into hiding. We'll find them soon enough. I have eyes and ears everywhere, and so far, they've stuck to the desert areas of the Southwest. That's where we're focusing our search. Don't worry, we've found them before, and we'll find them again, no matter where they try to run. Now, go get to work."

A minute after he dismissed them, Meade felt a buzzing in his pocket, from his personal phone, the one he always kept on silent so people wouldn't know he carried it. He locked the door to his office and checked the number.

The call was coming from Oscar Preston, a surveillance-photo analyst working for a private security firm contracting with the Pentagon. Oscar worked on a top-secret project studying photos of the UFOs that had been in a search pattern in the stratosphere for the past few years. He acted as one of Meade's back channels for intelligence. The government couldn't be trusted to give him all the information he craved.

"General Meade? We need to talk." Oscar sounded worried, panicked even.

"What's the matter?" Meade asked.

"Not on the phone. Meet me at the parking garage for the Capitol Mall, third floor, in an hour. This is really big. We've been getting it all wrong." Oscar hung up.

An hour later, Meade was waiting at the rendezvous point. He had changed into civilian clothes and was wearing sunglasses to obscure his identity. A light summer sports coat hid the 9mm automatic pistol in a shoulder holster on his left side. He had learned in several theaters of war that it always paid to be careful.

Meade scanned the parking lot for anyone who might be eavesdropping but saw no one. Oscar was as careful as he was, and he needed to be. Whenever Oscar wanted to speak with him in private, he always had some information to pass on that the higher levels of government thought Meade shouldn't know.

Oscar was a reliable source of information and knew when to reveal secrets and when not to. He was no Edward Snowden, fleeing the country and broadcasting government secrets to the whole world. Oscar knew just whom to give information to in order to keep in place the complex system of checks and balances that ensured a stable government that could defend the nation. Snowden had fired his shot and had no more ammo. He'd lost his security job and couldn't even come back to the United States without being arrested for treason. Oscar Preston was a quieter form of rebel and would remain useful for years.

Meade stood nonchalantly next to a car he pretended to be his, fiddling with his phone so any casual observer would think he was texting. He kept his eyes and ears open.

Oscar's car came up the ramp and slowly passed him. Meade didn't even look up as he drove by. Oscar parked on the opposite end of the level. Meade put away his phone and walked to a point well away from the car but in sight of it. After a minute, Oscar joined him.

"So what do you have for me?" Meade asked, eyeing the intelligence analyst.

Oscar was a civilian contractor and out of shape. His face was sweaty and pale, and he breathed heavily. The poor guy looked as though he had just run a mile. Meade guessed that was from panic, not exertion.

"It's amazing. I don't know who did it, but they've pulled one over on us."

"Who? What did they do?"

Oscar was about to speak but fell silent, giving a passing pickup truck a nervous glance.

Then he said, "This is too public. We should have picked a more private place."

"We've used this spot a dozen times before, and there's never been a problem. Now, tell me what's the matter."

Oscar put his fingers on his temples and shook his head. "I can't believe they did it. I've suspected for a while, but it took some time to get some proof. Here, look at this." Oscar pulled a manila envelope out of his case. A moment later, he stuffed it back in the case as another car passed.

"Relax, Oscar. If you act nervous, you'll attract attention. The average civilian won't even look at you if you act normally."

Oscar let out a breath and pulled the envelope out of his case again.

Just then, another car passed by slowly. Meade ignored it until, out of the corner of his eye, he saw the passenger-side window come down. The muzzle of an Uzi poked out.

"Down!" Meade shouted, grabbing the analyst.

Too late. The machine gun roared. Oscar's body flailed, his arms jerking above his head. Meade ducked behind a concrete pillar as he felt the heat of a bullet graze his side.

Once safe behind the pillar, he whipped out his pistol and glanced around the corner. The car was still there. He ducked back out of sight an instant later as the submachine gun fired a burst in his direction, chewing up the edge of the pillar and breaking off fragments of concrete that shot out across the parking lot, chipping windows and dinging the sides of cars.

Meade ducked, rolled to the other side of the pillar, and fired from a prone position. He didn't have a good angle of fire, but four bullets punching through the doors and windows of the gunmen's car changed their attitude pretty quickly. The driver slammed on the gas, and the vehicle peeled out.

After rising to one knee, Meade put the remaining rounds of his clip into the back of the vehicle. He couldn't see whether he'd hit anyone. The driver was still alive, in any case, because the car swerved around the corner, sideswiped another pillar with a loud crunch of metal on concrete, and roared away.

Hurrying over to Oscar, Meade immediately saw he was dead. Oscar's eyes were bugged out and his mouth open, as if he was still in panic, forever. The manila envelope Oscar had tried to give him lay in a widening pool of blood. Meade picked it up and hurried away. Oscar was beyond all help, and to hang around would only lead to uncomfortable questions. Plus, he had to get out of there in case those guys came around for another pass.

He glanced at the manila envelope, soaked and dripping with Oscar's blood. Whatever it contained, someone was willing to kill a Pentagon analyst to keep it hidden.

They were willing to kill a general too.

Chapter 9

July 25, 2016, MARRAKESH,
MOROCCO
12:30 P.M.

Otto couldn't decide if jetlag was making him hallucinate or if he really was walking through a traditional Arab *medina*, or market, in Marrakesh.

He and Grunt had passed under a soaring Arabian-style arched gateway that pierced the medieval city wall and found themselves in maze of winding streets and alleys. Some lay open to the punishing North African sun, but most were mercifully sheltered by a roof of reeds, which let little slats of light through the gaps between them to illuminate their way.

The medina was a sensory overload. Crowds of people jostled him, looking as though they came from all parts of the world and wearing everything from the latest Western fashions to traditional clothes Otto had never seen outside of a movie.

Many of the men wore what Grunt told him was called a *djellaba*, which kind of looked like an oversized shirt reaching down to just above the feet. It looked loose and comfortable, a good adaptation to the Moroccan heat, and they came in all colors from dirt brown to canary yellow.

Just in front of him, an old man hobbled along, wearing an embroidered skull cap, green-and-white striped flannel djellaba, and pointed yellow slippers. Next to him walked his son, who looked about Otto's age and wore jeans, a flashy pair of Nikes that were probably knockoffs, and a leather jacket. That seemed to be the uniform for guys his age. All the young guys who looked like they had any money wore leather jackets and seemed proud of them. He hoped that made them happy. They must have been boiling.

The women dressed in all styles, too. Some wore jeans and loose long-sleeved shirts with their luxuriant black hair uncovered and flowing past their shoulders. Others wore plainer, baggier clothes and a headscarf, and Otto saw a few women covered in heavy black cloth from head to toe, with only a thin slit in their veil to see out. They even wore black gloves. Otto couldn't figure out how they could stand it. Even in a T-shirt, he still felt the heat. They must have been even hotter than the guys.

The faces came in as wide a variety as the clothing. People who looked like Arabs seemed to be in the minority there. Others looked almost European or Jewish or had white skin but African features. Others were black African. Many more were a mixture of all of those races. Otto figured Jaxon would feel right at home. The people spoke to each other in Arabic, a strange language that Otto was sure he could never learn. Sometimes he caught snatches of conversation in French and Spanish too, plus other languages he couldn't identify, let alone understand. He felt very out of place. They hadn't seen another Westerner for a while. Grunt was leading them deep into the traditional quarter.

Pressing through the throng, Otto was dazzled by shops on either side of the covered street. Most were tiny little spaces barely wide enough to stand in, but they held so much stuff. One had a hundred different types of olives heaped in big bowls. Another was covered floor to ceiling in embroidered slippers that came in every color imaginable. Next to it was a spice shop that made Otto sneeze. Strange-colored powders sat in tidy cones. A woman was ordering several different powders, which the proprietor, an old man with a long white beard and matching skullcap, ladled into little plastic bags with a spoon.

Poorer vendors who couldn't afford a shop had laid out their merchandise on blankets by the side of the street and hunched beside them, calling out their wares. One guy sold nothing but scissors. Another had a row of battered old cell phones and chargers. Next to him was a man selling some rusty old tools and a pile of onions. Otto wondered if those folks could make a living.

Grunt walked beside him, wearing a *kaffiyeh*, a cloth that covered the head and neck, kept in place by a little cord around the head.

"You look like a local," Otto joked.

"I look like a damn tourist. Moroccans don't wear the kaffiyeh. Only the Arabs further east do. But it keeps anyone from seeing my ink. Tribal tattoos kind of stand out here. I don't want anyone to identify me."

"Who's going to know you here?"

"Mind your own business."

Grunt had been edgy when they took off from JFK International Airport in New York, finally taking a sleeping pill in order to relax and then snoring his way across the Atlantic. That kept Otto awake the whole flight. As the landing gear hit the tarmac at Marrakesh airport, Grunt's eyes snapped open. He'd been irritable ever since.

Now there they were, getting baked in the noontime heat of North Africa.

Too bad I can't ditch him for a while.

Impossible. To do that would mean heading out alone, and he had no idea where he was at the moment. The Atlantis Allegiance had broken up and taken three different flights from three different airports. Vivian and Jaxon traveled together as mother and daughter while Yuhle, Yamazaki, and Edward went on another flight. Those three checked in at different times and had reserved seats in different parts of the airplane.

Grunt and Otto, traveling as father and son, had landed first. They had to get someplace quiet and private to stay, away from prying eyes.

"Quiet and private" didn't seem to be available in Morocco because everyone watched everyone else. Between the little shops stood narrow, dim cafes where men sat idly watching the passing crowd while sipping tall glasses of steaming mint tea. Other people, children or grown men but never grown women, stood by the side of the street, not doing anything other than stare as people passed by. The shopkeepers did the same. Otto wondered which ones might be some of the many plainclothes policemen Grunt had warned him about. Apparently, they were everywhere. Otto hardly saw any regular cops except for the two burly guys at the gate, toting machine guns, and the small army guarding the airport. There had even been a couple of tanks parked outside.

He wished he had a tank to plow through the cloud of street hustlers buzzing around them. Young guys in leather jackets tugged at Otto's arm, ("You want hashish, mister? Good price.") or older, more respectable men waved flashy fake Arab daggers in front of his nose or little handmade leather camels ("Genuine Moroccan quality"). One guy in a tattered old djellaba plunked a fez on Otto's head.

"Thanks, now you look as dumb as me," Grunt said. "I feel much better now."

Otto laughed. "How much for the fez, buddy?"

The Moroccan smiled. "Two hundred dirham, my friend. Very good quality."

Twenty bucks? Not so bad. Otto handed him the money. The man took the bills, touched them to his forehead, and disappeared into the crowd.

Suddenly, Otto was surrounded by a dozen salesmen, all pushing products into his face.

"You've done it now, Pyro. They're like piranhas, and you just bled into the river. Oh, by the way? You paid way too much for that fez. You're supposed to haggle here."

Otto barely heard him over the shouts about the fine quality of the trinkets being dangled in front of him. Every single cheap bauble was "antique," "rare," and "handmade." Otto could barely walk. They kept getting in his way and blocking his view.

"Imshi!" Grunt bellowed.

The salesmen scattered.

"What did you say?" Otto asked.

"It means 'get lost.' I'll teach you more later."

"You speak Arabic?"

"I'm a bit out of practice, but yeah. Why, you think I'm too dumb to learn a foreign language?"

Otto grinned. "Don't make me answer that. Are we there yet?"

"Almost."

They were following directions Edward had given them to some private hotel deep in the medina, which had a trustworthy owner. How Edward knew about it when he hardly ever left his trailer was a mystery. Otto figured he'd gotten a tip from one of his online hacker friends. That guy had no social life in the real world but seemed to know everybody worth knowing in the hidden corners of the Internet.

Edward had given them written instructions, but the streets had quickly turned into a maze, and Otto had no idea where he was or how to get back to the main gate. Grunt strode forward, hardly hesitating at the intersections.

"You know where we're going?" Otto asked, shooing away another guy offering him hash.

"Never been to this place Edward knows, but it's in the residential area a bit behind Koutoubia Mosque, and I know where that is."

"So you've been to Marrakesh before?" Otto asked.

"Years ago."

"How can you remember your way through all this?"

"The key to walking in the medina is 'Don't think, and let your feet lead you. They remember.' Some old fart in Damascus taught me that, and it's always worked. Here we go."

"Damascus? You were in Syria?"

"For a while, yeah," he said and let out a loud breath.

"Is there any dangerous part of the world you haven't been to?"

Grunt stopped to think. One of the hash dealers who had been tagging along behind them didn't stop in time and bounced right off him. He staggered away. Grunt didn't seem to notice.

"Somalia. Thank God I've never been to Somalia."

The mercenary indicated a narrow side street that had no shops, only the bare metal doors of the houses. There were no ground floor windows, and the upper windows were always small and placed high up. People apparently liked their privacy, and that made the streets look like canyons.

Grunt stopped at an arched wooden door carved with ornate arabesques and studded with brass knobs turned a dull green by age. He grasped a big bronze knocker at the center of the door and rapped it loudly.

Otto looked around the doorway curiously. "Hey, there's no sign here. You sure this is the right place?"

The door opened, and a small man in an old, worn pair of slacks and a sports jacket greeted them in English.

"Welcome to my place. You are Mr. Sanders and his son?"

"That's right," Grunt said. "The others will come later."

"I am Mohammad el Aoufi. Come in, come in."

They entered, and Mohammad closed the thick door with a loud thud. He locked it then locked a second lock then slid a heavy steel bolt across it.

The interior couldn't have been more different from the chaos outside. Mohammad led them through a dark, cool hallway to a sun-drenched courtyard with a fountain in the middle. No water flowed in it, but the blue-and-green tilework shone brilliantly in the noonday sun beaming straight down on it. Otto looked up and saw the hotel had three stories, each with a row of windows looking onto the courtyard, their green grillwork shutters closed against the sun. High above in the pale, painfully blue sky wheeled the distant silhouettes of birds.

"Buzzards," Grunt said, pointing up at them. "They're waiting for you."

"Har har," Otto said then dropped his voice to a whisper. "Why is there no sign on the door?"

"Because this is a hotel for people who want to disappear for a while," Grunt whispered back.

Mohammad waited at a respectful distance until they were done talking and then approached. "You need how many rooms?" Mohammad asked.

Grunt turned to Otto. "You and your girlfriend sharing a room?"

"Um, no."

Grunt gave him a playful slap upside the head. "You're an idiot."

"I don't think she's ready for that."

"Oh, I'm just kidding, Pyro. I mean, you are an idiot, just not about this. She's got a lot on her mind, and you have to take it slow with her."

Grunt turned to Mohammad and told him what they needed. Grunt and Otto would double up, as would Vivian and Jaxon. Otto was surprised to hear Yuhle and Yamazaki would share a room but decided not to ask. Edward, of course, got his own room. The poor guy couldn't handle too much human contact. The transatlantic flight was sure to take a lot out of him.

Mohammad led them up a winding staircase of intricate green tile to a dark concrete hallway that echoed with their footsteps. A few colorful blankets and old tourist posters of Morocco hung here and there to break up the dirty, flaking white paint on the walls.

Their room was basically a concrete box, cool and dark after the powerful sunlight that had hammered down on them when they got off the plane, as well as the stuffy heat of the medina streets. Two creaky beds took up much of the room, along with a tiny table carved in the Arabian style and a couple of rickety chairs. Otto peered into the bathroom, eyeing the patched and kinky pipe leading out of the wall to the sink and shower. A rusty old water heater was bolted on a little wooden shelf on the wall.

"The bathroom work okay?" he asked Mohammad.

"No problem."

"I mean, it's…" Otto made a significant gesture towards the puddle under the pipe, growing a little bit larger every three seconds with a steady *drip drip drip*.

Mohammad seemed unfazed. "No problem. Enjoy your stay. We have no rules here except do not speak to the other guests. They will not speak to you. If anyone you don't know tries to speak with you, please come see me, and I will handle it."

With a bow, Mohammad left their room, closing the door behind him. Otto noticed the door had a regular lock, a chain, and a heavy deadbolt, plus a peephole.

"Hell of a place Edward got us." Otto chuckled.

"It's safe. Edward wouldn't stay here if it wasn't."

"We need to get some bottled water." Otto went into the bathroom.

"Nah, the water is fine here. I've drunk city water all across Morocco and never had a problem. Your mileage may vary.

Watch it in the villages, though. You don't want to get sultan's revenge."

Otto turned the tap on the sink. And turned it. And turned it some more. The pipes groaned and rattled, but nothing came out.

Suddenly, there was a loud *splursh*, and a gush of water shot out of the tap, splashing off the sink to soak his T-shirt.

"Damn, Pyro, you sick already?" Grunt called from the bedroom.

"That was the sink, not me."

"Good, the United Nations has rules against poison gas."

"Very funny."

How long am I going to have to share a room with this guy?

On second thought, Otto realized he actually was glad Grunt had changed his mind. The danger they had faced in Arizona and California would be nothing compared to what they would be up against in Morocco. He still didn't know why Grunt had had a sudden change of heart. He knew better than to ask, though.

Otto turned the flow down to a decent level and washed his hands and face. The long walk through the city had left him feeling gritty.

He'd spotted the Atlas Mountains from the taxi as they came in from the airport. The huge peaks stood not far south of town, and south of them lay the Sahara Desert. Here the land was fairly lush, with a few olive trees and some farms in the countryside around Marrakesh. That wasn't what he had pictured when he'd thought of North Africa. He'd thought it was all desert.

After he washed, he opened the little shuttered window in the bathroom. It looked out over an alley so narrow he could almost lean out and touch the opposite wall. Beneath him, a man was leading a string of donkeys laden with burlap sacks. Suddenly, a long, mournful wail echoed down the alley, followed by a beautiful song in Arabic, its words flowing together or stretching out as the singer held onto a single note over a syllable.

"There's a concert on somewhere," Otto called to Grunt.

"That's the Muslim call to prayer, Pyro. That guy who sings it is called a *muezzin*. They practice that song all their lives. They used to sing it from the minaret, those towers the mosques have, but now they just sit inside with a loudspeaker. Glad you like it, because you're going to get woken up by it every morning at dawn."

"Dawn?"

"The Muslims pray five times a day, and the first prayer time is just before sunup."

The muezzin was joined by another from a mosque farther away, and their songs mingled.

"You ready to go?" Grunt asked.

"Where to?"

"Got to see a man about a camel, and you're my backup."

"A camel?" Otto asked, coming out of the bathroom.

"Jesus, Pyro, you got to take everything literally? No, we have to get some supplies, and I know the man who's got what I need."

"Do you know a lot of people here?"

"If I don't know them, I know somebody who does. There's no six degrees of separation in Morocco. It's three at the most."

They headed back into the street, passing through part of the main market again before swerving off down a tiny alley littered with trash. A gangly kid, not more than fourteen, sat on the ground. He was caked in dirt, his clothes and skin black with grime, his bare feet even nastier. The kid stared blankly at the opposite wall as he held a plastic bag to his face, inflating and deflating it as he breathed.

As they passed by him, Otto turned back and stared. "What's he doing?"

"Glue sniffer," Grunt said, shaking his head. "It's a cheap high, and a lot of the homeless kids get into it. If I catch you trying it, I'll kick your ass."

"No chance of that."

"Good. Stick with lighting fires. It's much healthier."

"Enough already! So doesn't anyone help those kids?"

"Some Moroccan doctors started a clinic for them, but there are too many to manage. Lots of kids from broken homes or dirt-poor villages end up in the big cities, looking for work or a chance to make it to Europe. Some end up like that kid. There must be thousands of them."

"Damn."

"This isn't the States or Europe, Pyro. No safety net here. Lots of people don't have anything. It's one of the reasons rebel groups and Islamist factions can get a foothold. When people are desperate, they'll do all sorts of stupid stuff."

Yeah, like set fire to the neighbor's barn.

Otto felt a deep sense of shame. Sure, his parents didn't give a damn about him or each other. They were always drunk or spending the night with someone else, but at least Otto had grown up in a warm house with food on the table and a school to go to. If he had ended up so maladjusted just from that situation, what would have happened to him if he had grown up half starving in Africa? He could have ended up like that kid back there or toting a machine gun with some nutcase Islamist group.

They passed down an even smaller alley. Otto looked nervously around him. After the press and noise of the market, he found the solitude disturbing. This looked like the sort of place where people could disappear.

"Here we go," Grunt said at last. He stopped at a blank metal door that didn't look any different from any of the others they had passed. He knocked twice then three times then twice again.

A little window opened up in the door, covered on the inside by mesh, which would keep anyone from sticking a gun inside.

Damn, I'm beginning to think like Grunt, Otto thought ruefully.

A narrow-eyed Moroccan man with a thin scar across one side of his chin stared at them for a moment before saying something in Arabic. Grunt replied in the same language.

The window slammed shut, and there was a rattling of chains and snapping of bolts.

The door opened onto a dark, narrow hallway. A man stood at the far end, holding an assault rifle.

As the guy at the door closed it behind him, Grunt took off his kaffiyeh, revealing the tribal tattoos that snaked across his neck and bald scalp.

The doorman's face lit up. "Malcolm!" He embraced Grunt and gave him a kiss on each cheek, something Otto had seen men do there. Otto hoped he wasn't going to get the same treatment.

Malcolm? How many names does this guy have? Oh wait, he boasted that he had seventeen. Wonderful. I think I'll just call him Grunt. It fits.

The doorman and Grunt had a quick conversation in Arabic before turning to Otto.

"I'm Ahmed," the doorman said. "Come."

He led them down the hall past the guy with the assault rifle. Otto nodded to him and got a cold stare in return. Taking a right, they passed down another short hall and entered a large room with a couple of low, battered couches and rugs on the floor.

Leaning on the couches and lined up on the floor were dozens of guns of all descriptions, everything from small hideaway automatic pistols to hefty machine guns.

Otto gaped. "You took me on a shopping trip to an arms dealer?"

"What did you think, Pyro, that we were going out for ice cream?"

Otto gave the room another look. "I don't see any Tasers."

"They don't do Tasers in this part of the world," Grunt said, reaching down and picking up a rifle. "Try this one on for size."

Otto handled it uncertainly. His uncle had taken him to a shooting range a couple of years before, but that was the only time he'd ever fired a real gun. He'd already been in fights with people shooting at him, but he always had his Taser or flash-and-smoke grenades. He'd never had to use lethal force. He wasn't even sure he could.

Otto thought back to the fight at the abandoned gas station. He'd complained that he wanted some real grenades to fight General Meade's agents. It didn't seem fair that they were trying to kill him and he was only trying to blind and stun them. But what if he really had some explosive grenades? Could he have used them, and how would he have felt about it afterward? He didn't want to kill anyone, but if people were trying to kill him or kidnap Jaxon or hurt anyone else in the Atlantis Allegiance, wouldn't he be forced to sooner or later?

Otto glanced at Grunt. The mercenary acted as if killing people was nothing more serious than smashing a window or driving over the speed limit. Otto couldn't help but notice, though, that Grunt always tried to avoid using his gun if he could, and he never bragged about his war exploits like some veterans he'd met. While Grunt might have been a killer, he didn't relish that status.

Grunt put a hand on his shoulder. "Don't worry, Pyro, it won't bite. We've had it easy, but now we're in a tough part of the world, and we'll probably end up in a lot tougher places than this. It's time to step up to the plate. You're in the major leagues now."

Otto stared at the gun in his hand, feeling a growing sense of dread. He wished he was back in Little Leagues. He didn't like how this was going at all.

Chapter 10

July 28, 2016, MARRAKESH,
MOROCCO

6:30 A.M.

Jaxon couldn't believe she was up so early. Back in the States, she woke up as late as possible. Sometimes, she felt like not getting out of bed at all.

In Morocco, though, she got up with the dawn call to prayer. The sweet singing brought her out of a restful slumber into a strange, exotic land still half asleep in the predawn light. A blissfully cool breeze blew through her latticed window to greet her as she got out of bed. She stood in front of it, letting it blow over her body, enjoying it while it lasted. Within a couple of hours, it would be warm. Within four hours, the heat would flatten her.

The songs from the various minarets near and far faded to a close, and she looked out over the flat roofs and rusty satellite dishes of the city as the light grew. It was still quiet out there. Most people didn't seem to go to the mosque. Perhaps they prayed at home or at least pretended to. She'd seen a TV program about Saudi Arabia, showing religious police going around and checking that everyone said their prayers. They even banged on windows, shouting to people inside to get down on the floor and pray. People who didn't pray got hit with long wooden sticks. There didn't seem to be any of that here.

Occasionally, she could hear a neighbor open and shut a door or see the dark silhouette of a woman on a rooftop putting up the wash. Someone would call to a friend on the street. The rumble of a cart passing beneath her window told her one of the merchants was getting an early start to the market with his produce.

The city was waking up. If she wanted some privacy, she wouldn't have much time.

Jaxon grabbed her nunchucks and sai and went down to the courtyard. At that hour, it was always empty.

She started with the nunchucks, taking care to begin slowly. Her first couple of times trying them, she smacked herself in the head before she learned the trick of it. The chain between the two sticks had to bend with your body, moving with your curves as you swung it over your shoulder or your side. Right hand flip up over shoulder, left hand behind to grab, left hand flip up over shoulder, right hand to grab. Again and again, picking up speed.

Her tablet leaned against one of the tiled pillars, showing a video for an instructor going through the moves. She always left it on mute, partially so she didn't disturb anyone sleeping behind the windows above her and partially because she didn't want anything disturbing the peacefulness of that time. The only sounds she heard were the early-morning birdsong as sparrows flittered overhead, along with the rattle of the chain and the swish of the sticks as she spun them faster and faster around her body.

The morning routine calmed her, helping her start her day with a clear head. Being in such a strange place, it helped to have something of a routine. She was making progress with her weapons, and most of all, it gave her something to do.

She wasn't getting to do much else. Everyone had become overprotective of her. Grunt and Otto were off making contacts with some people in the underground, the two scientists were at the university talking with Moroccan experts, Vivian was acting as her personal bodyguard, and she hardly even saw Edward. Besides a bit of sightseeing with Otto and Vivian, she barely even got to go out.

Everyone told her she needed to keep out of sight since General Meade was still looking for her.

Looking for her here? Yeah, right! How was she supposed to find her people if she was stuck in the hotel all day?

She couldn't even talk to the other guests. The place had a strange policy that no one spoke to anyone they didn't know. The other people staying there passed her in the hallway without even glancing at her. One of them, who looked like some Arabian oil sheik with long, loose white robes over his big belly, had wandered into the courtyard one morning while she was practicing and had immediately turned around and walked away without a word.

Another time, she had been sitting in the lounge sipping some of the awesome mint tea Mohammad's wife Fatima made, and a thin guy in a cheap suit and an old-school fedora had sat down nearby and ordered a tea as well. They both drank in silence, neither looking in the other's direction or at the TV showing Moroccan news with a droning Arabian narrator giving the room its only sound. She understood that everyone went there for the privacy, but that gave the place a creepy edge.

As Jaxon went through her moves in the courtyard, the hotel around her slowly woke up. She heard a rattle of dishes coming from the kitchen and the footsteps of one of the other guests passing through to the lounge. The square of sky three stories above her had brightened, and she could already feel its warmth.

The video finished, and she put away her weapons with a sigh. She didn't have much to look forward to for the rest of the day—just sitting around in the room, watching movies on her tablet, drinking tea alone in the lounge, and maybe getting a walk with Otto after he finished hanging out with Grunt's creepy criminal friends. Jaxon was on the trip of a lifetime, and all she got to do was hide in the hotel.

She returned to the room to find Vivian primping in the bathroom.

"Off on a date?" Jaxon joked.

"I wish. No drinks with the girls either, not in this town. No, I have to see someone about something."

You mean you're off doing something cool while little old me has to stay safe in the hotel?

Vivian came out of the bathroom. She looked gorgeous, as usual. "Sorry I can't be a better roommate and spend some more time with you. I have too much to do. So why are you sharing a room with me instead of your boyfriend?"

Jaxon blinked. That was a quick change of subject. "He hasn't been my boyfriend for that long."

"It's okay to wait, honey."

"It's not just that, but... there kinda was someone else. When I thought I'd never see Otto again, I was heartbroken, but then I accepted it. Then there was this other guy. I mean, we never really were officially boyfriend and girlfriend, and now I kinda regret it."

Vivian gave her a sympathetic smile. "Must have been tough not to get to say goodbye."

Jaxon's eyes filled. Vivian put a hand on her shoulder.

"Oh honey, we know this is hard for you. We asked you to walk away from your whole life."

Jaxon shook her head. "There was nothing worth missing in my old life, but that's not why I'm crying. He got murdered."

The story came out of her like a waterfall: her fight with her neighbors, her solo trips to bad parts of town, meeting up with Brett doing the same thing, and that last terrible fight, where he disappeared and ended up dead in a dumpster.

Vivian gave her a hug. That time, Jaxon didn't resist.

"That's terrible, honey. I've lost some good friends in the field, too. At least he was fighting for what's right."

Those last words came out with a note of regret. Jaxon squeezed her arm.

Vivian wiped the tears from Jaxon's eyes. "Chin up, girl. You can honor his memory by finding what you came for and stopping General Meade. He's out after all your people, and they won't be safe until he's gone. Speaking of, I got to see to one part of that plan right now. Sorry to run, honey, but I really got to go. You can't be late with the kind of people I'm meeting. Stay out of sight in the hotel. I know it's boring, but it's the safest thing. By the way, Edward wanted to see you."

Within a minute, Vivian was gone. Jaxon sat on the edge of her bed, feeling glum. So much was happening around her, and she didn't even get to be part of it. Forcing herself to get up, she headed over to Edward's room. That would be the last bit of socializing she'd get until evening.

Edward's room looked as though he had moved the mess of his trailer across the ocean to Morocco. His room had a large desk covered with three computers. Other equipment hummed and blinked their lights in the corners of the room. The rest of the place was covered in junk—dirty socks, empty candy wrappers, and half-filled bottles of flat Coke. He kept complaining that nobody could get Mountain Dew in Morocco and that he was stuck drinking "the weak stuff." Jaxon wrinkled her nose, wishing Edward would shower more often.

He greeted her nervously at the door before hurrying back to his computers.

"I downloaded some more videos for you," he said, looking at the floor. Edward never looked right at her. "Sorry it took so long, but it was five hundred gigs, and the satellite uplink here is terrible."

"You downloaded me five hundred gigs of video? I'm going to be practicing until I'm sixty."

"No, it's not all what you asked for. I found a torrents site that had videos for pretty much every martial-arts weapon. I downloaded them all. If I downloaded just something on nunchucks and sai, it might get flagged by a spybot."

"Huh?"

Sometimes, Edward sounded as though he was speaking another language.

"You bought those weapons from that guy in Chinatown. Isadore probably noticed. She'll realize you're going to teach yourself how to use them, so General Meade probably set up a spybot to flag anyone downloading that stuff. Of course, lots of people download martial-arts videos, so it will only make an alert if someone only downloads videos for those two particular weapons."

"Um, okay. Thanks."

It sounded ridiculous, like some crazy conspiracy theory. Jaxon couldn't decide whether Edward was paranoid or she was naïve. Maybe both were true. Her idea of reality seemed to have been taken apart piece by piece in the past few months. She didn't know what to believe anymore.

Edward offered her a thumb drive.

As she turned to leave, he blurted, "Do you like the hotel?"

Jaxon turned back to him and found him blushing.

"I-I found it for you, I mean for us. All of us."

"Yeah, it's great."

Edward looked flustered. "It's pretty expensive, but it's safe. I figured you'd like the private courtyard."

"I do, thanks," Jaxon said, softening her tone. Because Edward was so brittle, she always had to take care when talking to him. "Glad we're getting the four-star treatment, or at least what passes for it here. So you were going to tell me where your money comes from?"

Edward shifted in his seat and blushed. The poor guy always seemed tense around her. She wondered if that was because she was a girl or because he was actually tense all the time.

"Well, yeah. I don't want you to think I'm a criminal or something. I mean, I break laws, but only the bad laws."

Jaxon tried very, very hard not to roll her eyes. That would only fluster him even more, and she wanted to hear his answer even if it was some sort of self-justifying BS. She'd heard plenty of that before.

"You see, I work for another organization, too," Edward said. "I met them on the Darknet. No, don't look at me like that. It's not just for criminals. A lot of political groups meet there too because they're harder to trace. Democratic activists in countries with dictatorships, stuff like that. Social reformers, too. Anarchists. Transhumanists. Vigilantes. I got a job with the last group. It's called Operation Lifeline. They use crowdfunding to hire people like me to take down illegal websites, both on the Darknet and on the regular web."

"What kind of sites?"

Edward let out a sigh. "Child pornography and child trafficking."

Jaxon's stomach turned.

Edward went on. "Some of the Operation Lifeline sponsors are millionaires. They offer a lot of money, more if you can find out user information, and even more if your work leads to a conviction. I'm very good at what I do. I find these sites"— Edward grimaced—"and hack into them, planting spyware on them. When a user logs on, they get tracked. Then I have their IP number, the unique code each computer has. After that, it's usually pretty easy to hack into their computer, turn on their webcam, and take a photo of them, time stamped for the same time they're accessing the illegal website. That's enough to get a conviction. The information gets sent to the FBI as well as Operation Lifeline. I've got it mostly automated on that computer over there in the corner. I've probably caught ten or twelve perverts today already. I'll check later this afternoon. That means a few grand."

Jaxon put her hand on his. Edward flushed and yanked his hand away.

"You're a hero," Jaxon said.

"Heroes don't ask for pay," he grumbled.

"Those FBI agents you contact get paid too, but they're still heroes. I think what you're doing is noble. But why did you pick..."

She let her words trail away. She was about to ask why he picked that line of work since it so obviously upset him, but when he turned away and his whole body started shaking, she knew the answer to her question.

"So I hope you like the hotel," Edward mumbled. "And, um, I put your CPS records on there too, in case, you know, you want to look at them or something."

"You saw my CPS records?"

Edward looked flustered. He took a minute to get a response out. "I had to so I could track you. I needed the Grants' address."

Jaxon stared at the thumb drive. She hadn't read those documents in a long time. She had never seen the point of reading about the past when she didn't have any future to look forward to.

Now, she felt different. She was part of something bigger. Her family had given her up, disappeared, but she still had her people.

And here she was, on the other side of the world, looking for them.

"Thanks, Edward."

The hacker nodded and turned back to his computer. He took a slug of Coke and started typing like mad. As he got into a groove, he seemed to grow a bit. His spine straightened a little, and he got an expression on his face that, while not quite confident, at least didn't look beaten anymore. He always looked better facing a screen than facing a human being.

He glanced over and saw Jaxon hovering by the door. "Don't worry about what they say in those things." Edward gestured at the thumb drive with a dismissive wave. "It's not you. It's just what the system thinks of you."

Back in her room, Jaxon turned the thumb drive over in her hands. Her social workers had sometimes offered to show the records to her and answer any questions she had about them, but it had been a long time since Jaxon had bothered. Too depressing, like she didn't have enough to be depressed about already.

That had been in her old life. She didn't know how her weird new life would turn out, but she was going to make damn sure it wouldn't end up like the old one.

She stuck the thumb drive into a laptop the Atlantis Allegiance had given her and found her CPS files. Scrolling down to the one with the oldest date, she opened it.

Abandoned Infant Report

Place of Discovery: Loretta Goldberg Clinic, San Francisco

Estimated Age: Three months

Sex: F

Race/Ethnicity: **Mixed, undetermined**

General Health: Excellent, well fed

Diseases/Infections: None

There they were—her vital statistics, her introduction to the world. The next document in the files, she knew, would show that the police had taken a print of her feet and checked it with all the state hospitals, only to find no match. Her mother had given birth either at home or out of the state. A later FBI report found no match nationally to the prints of any missing babies.

Jaxon's eyes strayed back to the second-to-last line. "Excellent, well fed."

She had forgotten about that. Maybe she had been too aloof to notice before what it really meant. It said so little and said so much. Her parents had cared for her. What had Isadore told her? A lot of her kind ended up criminals or suicide cases? Not her parents. They had loved her. They had taken proper care of her.

So why give her up? Had they been hunted like she was being hunted?

Jaxon felt relief and panic at the same time. Discovering that she hadn't been rejected by her parents felt like two giant boulders, sadness and cynicism, had fallen off her shoulders. Maybe she had been taking the wrong attitude all her life. Why hadn't she thought of this before?

Because you assumed you weren't special before. Now, you know you are.

But the fact that they'd loved her meant they hadn't wanted to give her up. They had been forced to for some reason. If those military agents wanted her as a weapon, they'd want all of her people as weapons. All the Atlanteans were being hunted.

And how long had this been going on?

She couldn't sit there in the hotel room anymore, waiting for someone to escort her through the streets. The answers she wanted were out there somewhere, and she should be the one finding them, not her new friends.

Jaxon got up and took some money and a card with the hotel address printed in English, French, and Arabic. She hurriedly wrote a note to Vivian on the back of her boarding pass and left it on her pillow. Jaxon hoped Vivian could read it. Her spelling always got worse when she felt nervous.

Locking the door behind her, she walked quickly downstairs, past the front desk as Mohammad merely nodded, and out into the streets of Morocco.

Chapter 11

July 28, 2016, ALBUQUERQUE, NEW
MEXICO
10:15 P.M.

General Meade sat late at his office.
He didn't feel safe at home. There in the
middle of a military base, at least he
wouldn't be shot at. Or would he?

The assassination attempt had left him
seriously rattled, the worst of it being that
he had no idea who had tried to kill him.
He didn't dare send out feelers through
his usual channels. Oscar's killing had
shaken up the entire Pentagon. When
a top-ranking intelligence analyst got
gunned down in a parking lot in broad
daylight, even the president heard about
it. Asking too many questions might lead

to people asking him questions, and he couldn't have that.

No one had come to talk to him about it. Apparently, he had gotten away clean. The only people who witnessed the shooting were he and the assassins.

And of course, the assassins knew he had been there.

General Meade felt like a sitting duck. The shooters had obviously known who he was, for they had been tracking Oscar. That meant they knew where he worked and probably where he lived. He had only been home once to pack a few things and move into a motel. He had to find one that would take cash—credit cards could easily be traced—so he'd ended up in a trashy motel in a bad part of town, the kind of motel where no one asks for ID when you check in and everybody minds their own business. He hoped nobody he knew spotted him there. Think of the scandal!

General Meade realized once again that his decision to never get married had been a good one. He had decided long before to devote his life to his career. Marrying someone and then running off to war zones for months or years at a time wouldn't have been fair. He'd seen plenty of military marriages break up over that. However, the war zone had come right to America, and he was taking fire in local parking garages.

There had been one woman who almost made him change his mind, though...

Meade shook his head to clear away his thoughts of a better past and the better future it had promised. He had to focus. After making sure the door to his office was locked, he retrieved the special plastic envelope in which he'd stored the photos Oscar had given him.

He'd spent hours laboriously cleaning the blood off them while trying to keep the paper as dry as possible. Even after all that work, he still didn't manage to get all the stains off. A lab tech with the proper equipment could have done a much better job in a tenth of the time, but he hadn't been able to risk showing the photos to anyone. Someone was willing to kill for them, someone within the military.

He spread the photographs out on the table and focused a bright lamp on them. As far as he could see, they weren't much different than any of the hundreds of other photos he had seen. Shiny metallic discs, larger black triangles, and huge cigar-shaped objects hovered above the clouds, some even higher in the upper stratosphere on the border of outer space. The images had been taken by spy planes and powerful ground-based telescopes.

General Meade took out a magnifying glass and studied them. What should he look for? Oscar had said something about their being fooled. Fooled about what? Could these not be extraterrestrial at all? Could the Russians or the Chinese have made them? Or some unknown, secret power?

He squinted at the photos one by one, taking in every detail. He wasn't an expert as Oscar had been, but he'd stared at enough intelligence photos to have a pretty good eye. The problem was that he didn't know what he was looking for. All the alien craft looked just the same as the others that had been tracked for the past several years, and the data printed on the edge of the photos showing coordinates, altitude, and speed were within the same general parameters.

He sifted through the photos one by one, then looked through them again.

Then one caught his eye. It showed a shiny metallic disc flying above some cirrus clouds, the wispy clouds that only form above eighteen thousand feet. Usually, the UFOs flew so high that no clouds would be in the picture at all. That made the photo unusual but not highly so. Other UFOs had been spotted at low altitudes, always the same flying-disc type. The cigar-shaped UFOs were considerably bigger and always stayed either in the upper stratosphere or in outer space. Scout vehicles and mother ships? Perhaps.

General Meade stared at the photo, trying to figure out what had caught his eye, what exactly was nagging him in the back of his mind.

His eyes drifted to the clouds. Something about them...

He hurried over to his computer and punched in his password to bring up the top-secret database of UFO images. Using the search engine, he narrowed down the thousands of pictures to only those with cirrus clouds in them, bringing the total down to a couple hundred. Then he went through them one by one.

He needed more than an hour to find it, but when he did, it was so obvious he nearly fell out of his chair.

The photo Oscar had given him was dated just three weeks before, and the photo on his screen dated more than two years before.

But the clouds were identical.

General Meade stared at his screen then at the bloodstained photo and back at his screen.

He couldn't deny it. The wisps of water vapor were the exact same shape. That didn't happen in nature. Clouds were like snowflakes, all different.

That meant the images were faked.

The UFOs in the two pictures were obviously different, with different angles and vectors and light conditions. The angle of light on the clouds was different too, as was the total brightness, but the shape was identical.

Whoever had faked the photos had gotten lazy and reused some cloud imagery, figuring no one would notice since the photos were from two years apart, and everyone would be focusing on the UFO anyway. The forger had assumed no one would catch it.

Oscar was smart enough to catch it.

Had been smart enough, Meade corrected himself.

General Meade looked at the other photos. Were these faked too? They must have been. Oscar would have checked, using the advanced analysis software in his lab, software Meade didn't have access to. Once he had spotted the first fake image, he would have suspected all of them and checked each one. Oscar must have been analyzing them for weeks, maybe even months, until he had assembled the stack of twenty images to show General Meade incontrovertible proof that the entire UFO hunt was a sham.

The general leaned back in his chair, closing his eyes and letting his breath out slowly. His world had just come apart. For years, he'd been following the UFO phenomenon, searching through everything the government had in its files. There had been so many false leads, so many silly eyewitnesses who'd seen Venus and thought it was an alien spacecraft. Even some of the government reports turned out to be meteors or experimental aircraft. But there had always been a hard core of cases, perhaps one percent, that couldn't be dismissed. And then the UFOs started flying through the upper atmosphere in what was obviously a search pattern, and the government had finally taken the threat seriously and begun monitoring them.

So was it all a fake? Did none of those craft exist? Were even those credible cases somehow falsified?

Who would want to fool the Pentagon? The images came from military installations, so it wasn't an enemy power unless they had managed to get a whole team of secret agents into a top-secret project. That seemed unlikely. The United States had certainly never managed to get access like that to an enemy power.

That left the United States government itself. One part of the government, perhaps a faction within the Pentagon, wanted the rest of the government to think an alien invasion was imminent.

General Meade rested his elbows on his desk and ran his hands through his hair, letting out a deep sigh. All he had worked for, all he had conspired to do, had been useless. He had enslaved Orion, a fellow human being, because he thought he needed to do so to defend the Earth. Damn it, he had even spoken with General Corbin about overthrowing the government in a military coup!

His ancestor, the famous General Meade of the Union army, the victor of Gettysburg, must have been spinning in his grave. Meade had fought the Confederacy to free the slaves and protect the Union, and there he was, 150 years later, enslaving Atlanteans and planning on overthrowing democracy, all because some trickster with a computer had made him believe in aliens!

He slammed a fist on his desk. They would pay—he'd make sure of that. All his efforts hadn't been for nothing. Sure, they had fooled him, but by fooling him they had spurred him to start the Poseidon Project and train Orion. Plus, he had the Grants and other agents at his disposal. Whoever was behind this had made a powerful enemy. He'd make them pay for their treason.

But who could it be? And why were they doing this? What did they have to gain?

His mind settled on General Corbin. He had been the commanding officer who had cleared the Roswell report for release into the top-secret Pentagon server. The military's initial report had long since been available, but there had been a second, more detailed report made a week after the 1947 crash, which had only just recently been uploaded onto the server. For those with eyes to see, that second report had been a bombshell.

There had been strange writing on the UFO that had crashed in Roswell, New Mexico, back in 1947, writing no one at the time could decipher. Only his lead scientist in the Poseidon Project, Dr. Jones, was able to figure out what it meant—it was part of the genetic sequence for the Atlantis set of genes.

That was enough to induce him to contact General Corbin. Soon, they were sharing information about aliens and Atlanteans. Not only that, they had agreed to do all they could to defend the Earth against the alien threat, up to and including overthrowing the democratically elected government in Washington in order to be able to mount a swift and decisive response again the invasion.

Had it all been a lie? Had Corbin falsified and planted that report, knowing that Meade would be so interested that he would get in touch? Had all this been to draw Meade and his Atlanteans into a plot to overthrow the government?

Perhaps Corbin wanted to be dictator. If he could fool the Pentagon into believing in an invasion from outer space, it would be easy to fool the general public. Half of them believed in UFOs already.

But when no invasion came, how would Corbin stay in power? Did he have some other trick up his sleeve? Or maybe Corbin was a dupe just like Meade had been. Should he contact him, try to draw him out? But if he had been behind Oscar's killing, that would be like walking into the lion's den.

Exhaustion tugged at him. He had been working hard all day, and this latest revelation was too much. His mind was a muddle and his thoughts unclear. He needed to go back to his motel and sleep on it. Maybe in the morning, things would be clearer.

Twenty minutes later, Meade pulled into the parking lot of his motel. It was just off the interstate, the kind of place truckers and traveling salesmen might stop after a long day on the road. The beds were creaky, the carpets all had cigarette burns, and the guy at the front desk looked like a drug addict. But it was a place no one would ever expect to find a general of the United States Armed Forces.

As he pulled into a parking space, he glanced around—nothing suspicious except for the drug dealer on the corner and the working girls hanging out next to the off-ramp.

It was a good thing there wasn't a Mrs. Meade. No woman he'd ever marry would be caught dead in that dump, and if she caught him there, she'd think he was having an affair. From the sound of it, the people in the room next to his certainly had been.

General Meade cut the engine and got out of his car, keeping his hand close to the pistol hidden beneath his civilian clothing. Gripping his key, he hurried to the door of his hotel room, which looked directly out on the parking lot. He scanned the area for potential trouble but didn't see anything beyond the usual. On his first night, he'd brushed off the drug dealer and the working girls, and they were leaving him alone. Briefly, he wondered what they thought of him. Why would anyone stay in this place, they must have wondered, if he didn't want their services?

As he came up to his room, he brushed his hand along the space where the door met the doorjamb. He had shut one of his own hairs between them, right next to the lock, a simple trick to catch the unwary prowler. Chances were, they wouldn't see the hair, and when they opened the door, it would fall to the ground. Its absence would signal that someone had entered his place without his permission.

The hair was absent.

Glancing around to make sure no one was watching, General Meade eased his 9mm automatic out of his shoulder holster and flicked off the safety. Edging away from the door so that if someone shot through it they wouldn't hit him, he inserted the key into the cheap lock. Any halfway decent burglar could've picked that lock in ten seconds.

He unlocked the door and pushed it open, tensing himself for the gunshot he felt was sure to come. When it didn't, he crouched and popped his head around the corner and quickly ducked back. No shots, and he hadn't seen a thing in the dim interior of his room. He stood up so as not to appear in the same spot a second time and popped his head around the corner again, leading with his gun.

No one.

General Meade reached around the corner and flicked on the light. The cheap room stood out starkly under the glare of the bare bulb—lumpy bed, battered side table, TV with adult channels, faded carpet, and the open door to the bathroom.

The only parts of the room he couldn't see were the floor on the far side of the bed, under the bed, and part of the bathroom.

Where would an intruder hide? Most likely the bathroom.

General Meade dove into the room and landed on the bed, rolling across it to the other side, where he was relieved to find no one hiding. As he landed on the floor, feeling brief satisfaction at the noise—revenge for the sleep deprivation his amorous neighbors had given him—he glanced under the bed. There were all sorts of horrors under that bed, but no hidden assassin. He felt oddly glad as he wouldn't have shoved his worst enemy under there.

That left the bathroom. General Meade trained his pistol on the doorway. He had expected someone to come leaping out, perhaps his friend with the Uzi from the parking lot.

He crept towards the half-open bathroom door. He could see only about half the room, including the chipped sink, part of the floor, and the mirror reflecting the entrance and parking lot. Nothing seemed out of place.

Wait, what was that on the floor? A bit of dirt, and not just the usual grime in that filthy place, but an actual little ball of soil that had obviously fallen off of someone's shoe. It hadn't been from him because he always tried to keep the place as clean as possible. Someone else had left it there.

Someone who'd hidden right behind that door.

General Meade rose, keeping his pistol trained on the doorway. He edged forward, trying not to make a sound.

Movement in the mirror made him spin around. A man was standing at the entrance to his motel room, an Uzi in one hand.

Meade put a bullet through his head.

As the assassin flew backward and flopped on the pavement, Meade spun again and ducked just as a shotgun blast tore through the room and ripped apart the wall behind him. Miraculously, he was unhurt and shot the second assassin, who had leapt out of the bathroom, right in the gut. The man crumpled onto the bathroom floor.

Meade kicked the man's gun away, glanced around the door to make sure no one else was lurking inside the bathroom, and ran to the door looking out over the parking lot.

No one was in sight. The neighborhood had gone deathly silent.

He rushed back to the man lying doubled up in agony on the bloody bathroom tiles.

Turning him over and sticking his 9mm in his face, Meade glared down at him. "Who sent you?"

The assassin managed a weak grin with bloody teeth.

Meade slapped him. "Who sent you?"

The assassin never stopped grinning as his eyes rolled up in their sockets and the last bit of light in them guttered out.

Meade didn't bother searching the bodies. They wouldn't be carrying anything that could identify them.

As the adrenaline from the fight wore off, Meade felt a prickling fear. The cops would come soon, even in that degenerate neighborhood. What would they say when they found a United States general in a cheap motel, standing over two dead bodies?

He had to get out of there.

Meade grabbed his things and stuffed them in his bag. Within seconds, he was out the door and to his car.

His car…

He paused in front of it. What if they had a backup plan? What if his car was booby-trapped?

Meade glanced around. He had to get out of there right away. He didn't have time to check for bombs, and in the half light of the parking lot, he might miss them anyway.

Then he saw the night manager's terrified face peeking out from the office window.

Meade leveled his pistol at him and strode over. Glancing to the left and right, he saw the dealer and the working girls had disappeared. A few cars were driving in the distance, but anyone who had been close enough to hear the shots had run away.

He stopped in front of the window.

"You. Out."

The manager cringed and scuttled out of the office.

"I won't tell anyone, I swear. I didn't see nothing."

Meade looked him over: sunken face, bloodshot eyes, rotten teeth, scrawny body. An obvious drug addict who had his mind together enough to hold down a job so he could support his habit. Nothing but human filth.

Meade handed him his car keys. "Open my car and start the engine."

"Wh-what?"

"You heard me. Do it."

The night manager walked unsteadily over to Meade's car, gasping as he saw the assassin's body sprawled in front of the motel-room door. As he got to the car, he paused, eyes growing wide.

"Did you see them doing anything to my car?" Meade asked.

"N-no."

"Unlock the door and start the engine," he ordered, backing away.

"B-but..."

"It's that or a bullet," Meade said, aiming the gun at his head.

Even then it took the guy a moment to decide. With a trembling hand, he put the key in the door and turned it. Meade and the night manager both winced, expecting an explosion. None came. Shaking like a leaf, the manager opened the door and sat in the driver's seat. He gave General Meade a pleading look.

"Don't make me do this."

"I need this car to get away. You have to check it."

"But—"

"Now."

The man put the key in the ignition and rested his forehead against the steering wheel. "I've done a lot of bad stuff in my life, but I don't deserve this," he whispered. He took a deep breath, sat up straight, and turned the ignition.

The car started normally.

The night manager lifted his eyes heavenward and raised his hands. "Thank you, God. I'll live a different life from now on." He stepped out of the car, leaving the engine running.

"I won't tell anyone a thing," he told General Meade. "I'm quitting this job and getting my life back together. I tried rehab once and it didn't work, but this time—"

General Meade pulled the trigger and blew the top half of the guy's head off.

He paused, looking down at the ruined body lying in front of him. "Sorry, but you could have identified me. There are bigger issues at stake."

Meade got into his car and drove away.

Chapter 12

July 28, 2016, MARRAKESH,
MOROCCO

8:45 A.M.

Jaxon strolled along a narrow lane near her hotel, her skin alive with a tingling excitement at having slipped away alone. She knew she would get lost among all those winding alleys and streets, but she decided to let go of her fear.

With that business card, she could always ask for directions and make her way back. Edward had also supplied each member of the Atlantis Allegiance with an untraceable phone bought on the street and supplied with enough prepaid credit to keep them going for a time. She could call one of the others to come get her.

At the moment, she had her phone turned off. She didn't want to talk to anyone—she wanted to explore. She felt kind of bad at cutting off the others when all they wanted to do was help her, but if they wanted to help her, they had to let her help herself.

The part of the medina she was passing through was less crowded than the bigger streets, but she still had to go slowly. People were walking leisurely, stopping to talk with anyone they knew by shaking their hands and kissing them on each cheek, or if the person was passing by too far away, a simple wave and a pat on the heart was enough. Jaxon liked that gesture. The people seemed friendly even though a lot of them looked poor or tired. Marrakesh, at least the little she had seen of it, didn't feel like a third-world country. The lights worked, the plumbing usually worked, and nobody seemed to be starving. Everything was a little ragged, though, like the beat-up old cars that belched exhaust in the bigger streets and the flaking paint on all the buildings, and she saw a lot of beggars and a lot of working people who looked pretty poor. It was more like a second-world country. Jaxon wondered if that was a real expression. People always talked about the first world and the third world, but she bet there were a lot of countries like Morocco that sort of fit in the middle.

The medina felt like its own little world, with countless alleys and shops and residential homes. Almost none of the streets were wide enough for a car, and most people walked.

Every now and then, the pedestrians had to squeeze against the wall or duck into a shop to avoid a motorcycle tooting down the lane or a rumbling little three-wheeled motorized cart delivering produce or gas canisters. Jaxon liked that the cars couldn't make it in there. The drive from the airport had been crazy, with crowds of cars and trucks speeding along and cutting each other off. Looking over the dashboard of their taxi, she felt as if she were in some sort of real-life video game. She had been worried that Morocco would be dangerous, but the only dangerous people she'd seen were the drivers.

To either side of the lane stood little shops or the stalls of craftsmen. In one, an old man with thick eyeglasses carefully cut leather into patterns for some sort of clothing while his neighbor sewed one of those giant brown cloaks the men wore despite the heat.

There were also the Moroccan equivalent of convenience stores, little wooden counters, always painted sky blue for some reason Jaxon couldn't figure out, piled high with candy, cartons of milk, and potato chips.

Jaxon spotted a carton of fruit juice at one of them. Feeling thirsty, she plucked up her courage and went over.

The man behind the counter, a hunched-over middle-aged guy with a salt-and-pepper beard and white skullcap, said something to her in Arabic.

"Um, can you speak English?" Jaxon reminded herself to get a phrase book if they were going to hang out in the area for a while.

The man looked surprised. "Yes, a little."

"How much for the fruit juice?" Jaxon asked, pointing.

"*Kam.*"

"What?"

"*Kam* means 'how much.'"

"Kam?"

"*Ashra darahim.* Ten dirham."

Jaxon grinned and pulled out a coin. If everyone acted that helpful, she wouldn't need a phrase book after all.

Someone tugged on her sleeve. Jaxon turned to see a plump older woman in a headscarf and a loose robe. The woman asked her something in Arabic.

"I'm sorry, I don't understand you."

The woman looked surprised and said something to the storeowner before chuckling and walking away.

"She says you look Moroccan," the storeowner said.

"Um, thanks."

"Are your parents from Morocco or from Algeria or Mali, perhaps?"

"No, California."

"Ah, there are many Moroccans in California! I have cousin who has restaurant in Los Angeles. Are you certain your parents are not Moroccan?"

"Not Moroccan, but close." Jaxon laughed as she walked away. Under her breath she whispered, "I'm Atlantean. Too bad no one seems to know what that means."

Sipping her fruit juice, which was warm but at least quenched her thirst, she studied the area she was walking through. Buildings rose three or four stories on either side, looking almost featureless with their whitewashed, grimy walls and little windows, almost always shut. The doors, some of ornately carved wood and others of blank metal, always stayed shut. The Moroccans appeared to be a private people.

She didn't feel threatened, though. All she knew about the Muslim world were the wars and massacres she saw on TV, but Marrakesh wasn't like that at all. Vivian had told her that, while it wasn't as safe as the better parts of Los Angeles, it was a lot safer than some of the neighborhoods where Jaxon and Brett used to hang out. The government was stable, and there wasn't a civil war on. That wasn't the case with the rest of the countries in North Africa.

Jaxon didn't even feel all that out of place. In fact, people didn't pay much attention to her at all. Otto and the scientists always got surrounded by people trying to sell them cheap tourist trinkets. She'd seen some locals carrying fezzes or curved Moroccan daggers or little leather camels, but none of them had come up to try to sell her that junk.

She scanned the crowd for faces like hers. The population was so mixed that she saw every race she could name, plus a few she couldn't, and a whole bunch of people who looked like a mixture of two or more races. That gave her confidence. She didn't stand out in Morocco as she had back home. In a population that diverse, no one was going to give her a weird look just because of her appearance. Even her clothes weren't all that different. She looked like a lot of the younger Moroccan women who dressed in Western styles.

Every now and then, though, a woman shrouded in heavy black cloth would pass by, her face invisible behind a veil, or Jaxon would spot a butcher's shop with a line of lambs' heads on display, or she'd pass an alley blocked by a row of men kneeling on prayer rugs and touching their foreheads to the ground, and she'd remember that while she might look as though she fit in, she was still a foreigner in a very foreign land.

Everything was brand new to her. She'd only been out of the hotel a couple of times on some amazing walks through the city. They'd seen a beautiful Islamic art pavilion all made of red tile next to a pool that reflected it and the Atlas Mountains looming behind it. Those mountains beckoned to her. Beyond them lay the desert and, Dr. Yamazaki had told her, perhaps more of her people. Otto and Jaxon had also gone to a giant town square called the *Jemaa el Fna*, where peddlers sold all sorts of spices and jewelry while jugglers and acrobats performed for the crowd.

She found the medina just as fascinating. That was where regular folks lived and worked, and behind some of those doors, some of her people must have been living. Jaxon kept searching the crowd, hoping to spot a black face with bright blue eyes. No luck. Apparently, the Atlanteans were rare there, too.

For two hours she wandered, the heat getting so bad that she had to get another carton of fruit juice. Once again, it was warm. She guessed those little blue convenience stores didn't invest in refrigerators. She had become thoroughly lost in the maze of the medina, but she didn't worry about that. All she focused on were the faces in the endless stream of people passing by. Someone like her had to live in the huge city.

Then, a woman's face caught her eye. She wore loose robes and a pale yellow, gauzy headscarf. Her face was exposed and showed dusky skin, wide cheekbones, and brilliantly blue eyes.

Jaxon stopped and stared. For some reason, Courtney's words came back to her. Those eyes really were pretty, especially when set off against dark skin.

The woman was walking toward her, carrying some vegetables in a plastic bag. She didn't even glance at Jaxon as she passed.

Jaxon hurried after her. "Excuse me? Do you speak English?"

The woman looked at her, obviously confused. Jaxon felt a spike of disappointment. She had almost expected the woman's face to light up as she hugged

Jaxon and brought her to a home of Atlanteans to have a big family reunion. She thought all she had to do was make contact and a lifetime of questions would be answered.

Instead, the woman gave her a bashful smile and said, "No English. *Parlez-vous français?*"

"Um, no."

The woman shrugged and said something in Arabic. She turned to go, and Jaxon got in front of her again.

"Don't you see it? We're the same people," Jaxon said, pointing to her face and then the stranger's. "Atlantean. You're Atlantean. I'm from Atlantis too. Well, our ancestors were, anyway."

The woman's expression showed she didn't understand. Then, to Jaxon's surprise, the woman took her by the hand and led her down one of the streets.

"Thank you!" Jaxon said. "I'm so anxious to meet other people like me. Do you know someone who speaks English? I have so many questions."

The woman simply nodded and took her around a corner and into a main street lined with jewelry shops. Brightly lit windows sparkled with gold and diamonds. Far ahead, the lane intersected a square or a bigger street, with an arch opening up into an area of blazing sunlight.

The woman repeated something three times, pointing toward that sunlit arch. Then she smiled and walked away.

"Wait!" Jaxon called.

The woman simply turned, smiled again, and pointed toward the arch.

Frustrated, Jaxon headed toward the end of the street. Maybe there was a neighborhood of Atlanteans over there. Yeah, that must be it! The woman couldn't speak English and was obviously in a hurry, so instead of taking her there herself, she had pointed the way.

Jaxon hastened her steps, weaving her way through the crowd as sweat trickled down her back. As she approached the arch, the heat got worse, the air heavy with spices and cooking as she passed some food stalls. After the shadowy streets of the medina, the sunlight blinded her. She shaded her eyes as she passed under the arch and came into the direct sunlight. The sun had risen high in the sky. Jaxon reckoned it must be almost noon. She'd been wandering the medina all morning.

Jaxon blinked as her eyes became accustomed to the light. What she saw made her heart sink.

She was in the *Jemaa el Fna*, the giant square with all the food stalls and performers and cafes. Tourist central. She and Otto had gone there a couple times and had seen no Atlanteans.

The woman had misunderstood. She had taken Jaxon for a lost tourist and directed her to the city's main landmark.

How could she not recognize the similarity in their faces? Wasn't it obvious?

The depressing answer dawned on Jaxon soon enough—the woman didn't know what she was, just as Jaxon hadn't known until the Atlantis Allegiance saved her. What if none of the Atlanteans knew their true history? What if all those centuries of hiding and running from persecution had destroyed the memory of where they were from?

Jaxon sighed. The square was way too hot—over a hundred. At least from there, she sort of knew how to get back to the hotel. She shook her head in frustration and headed back. Everybody was probably freaking out by then, so she figured she should probably get back.

She crossed the square, the sun pressing down on her, and entered another of the arched gates that led into the covered medina. Coming in from the sun, the shade seemed almost pitch black by contrast. She had to pause for a moment to let her eyes adjust. That gave her time to remember the way, and soon she was following alleys as they grew narrower and narrower, and the shops gave way to residential buildings.

When she was just a few minutes away from the hotel, lost in her own glum thoughts and sense of helplessness, she heard a strange fluting coming from one of the side alleys. Jaxon stopped and listened. The music had a shrill, tinny sound yet made a beautiful melody, one with a regular rhythm that she could follow along and anticipate. It was different from the haunting mosque music, earthier, like folk music.

The music got drowned out by a gaggle of young boys rushing into the alley, the leader pointing the way and shouting over his shoulder to his friends. The alley took a right turn just a few yards down, and within seconds they tore around the corner and disappeared. A few other children trickled into the alley as well, as well as a couple old men. They all went around the corner, too.

Curious, Jaxon paused at the intersection. The music continued, picking up volume.

"Why not?" Jaxon said with a shrug and followed the crowd.

Around the corner, the alley opened up into a small courtyard formed by old buildings with arched windows covered by complex wooden latticework. An ancient, crumbling fountain stood in the center. Unlike the one in her hotel, that one actually had water in it, burbling out to splash over intricate blue and green tiles.

Beside the fountain stood an old man in a faded yellow djellaba and cracked leather sandals. He was playing a strange wooden flute that flared out to a big bulb near the bottom before crimping back into a small airhole. In front of him sat three wicker baskets, and a few feet away from them, a half circle of old men and young boys, with a few shy girls sticking close to their brothers. Jaxon moved to the front row and sat down. A little boy next to her grinned up at her and said something in Arabic. Jaxon smiled back at him.

The man with the flute bent down, his knobby knees poking the sides of his djellaba, and waved the flute over one of the baskets as he played. Jaxon wondered what could be inside those baskets. The audience seemed fixated on them. One of the boys next to her nudged his friend and giggled, pointing at them.

With the end of the flute, the old man flicked the top of the basket off, and a cobra popped up. Jaxon flinched.

The snake stretched up, half its body out of the basket and the rest coiled within. The hood just below its head was spread wide open, and its forked tongue flicked in and out, barely an inch from the tip of the flute.

The old man began to rock back and forth, his flute rocking with him. The snake sat immobile, only its tongue moving. As the snake charmer continued to rock, the snake slowly uncoiled, lifting itself out of the basket. Its head rocked in time to the flute. Jaxon shuddered as the snake slid out of the basket and stopped just inches from the old man. It coiled up again, its head rising as the tongue flicked in and out, tasting the end of the flute.

Jaxon had heard that snakes coiled when they wanted to strike, shooting forward like a spring. Was this cobra about to attack?

Still squatting, the snake charmer shifted his feet and moved over to the second basket. Once again, he flipped the top of the basket off with the end of his flute to reveal another cobra. Then he shifted again and did the same with the third basket.

Within seconds, he had three deadly poisonous snakes coiled at his feet. His tune changed, and the snakes slowly stretched themselves out and started to move closely around him, forming a ring.

Jaxon tried to edge away but bumped into the legs of a man standing right behind her. The snakes were slithering only a couple of feet away from her. If they decided to attack, she would have nowhere to run. She glanced at the boys sitting to either side of her and saw their eyes had grown wide with wonder, their little mouths hanging open. They didn't seem to show much fear, though. Maybe they were too young to realize just how crazy the snake charmer was.

The old man put down his flute. As soon as the music stopped, the snakes stopped too, flicking out their tongues at the hem of his djellaba. He plucked one of the snakes off the ground, holding it by its middle as it bared its fangs and struck at him, its glossy body uncoiling like a whip.

The snake charmer had measured the distance perfectly, and the cobra could only reach to within a couple of inches of his face. The man stuck out his tongue so that he could almost lick the long, curved fangs of the poisonous serpent. He rocked back and forth, teasing the snake as it lunged for him, always missing by an inch.

Jaxon's eyes widened as the other two snakes slithered up the man's back. He looked over his shoulder at them with a smile and bent over to let them climb up more easily. Soon, they coiled around his neck, turning their heads to watch the crowd with beady black eyes. Meanwhile, the snake he held calmed down and froze in place, staring right at the snake charmer.

Slowly, the man stood straight, and Jaxon gritted her teeth at the thought of one of those snakes getting disturbed and biting him or springing off his shoulders to attack the front row. How good were Moroccan hospitals? She didn't want to find out.

The snake charmer looked right at her and smiled.

"Don't even think of making me part of your show," she told him.

He cocked an eyebrow. "American?" he asked.

"Yes."

"You have good time in Morocco?" he asked in heavily accented English.

"So far it's pretty cool except for the snakes. Could you maybe step back a little?"

He said something to the crowd in Arabic, and everyone laughed. Jaxon blushed. Was he making fun of her?

The old man seemed to remember he was in the middle of a show with three deadly snakes draped over him. He puffed out his chest, got a serious look on his face, and lifted the snake he held high into the air.

With the forefinger of the other hand, he touched the base of the snake's mouth. Jaxon tensed again. The guy was really pushing his luck.

He ran his finger down the snake's body, and everyone gasped as the cobra went as limp as a wet noodle. With a deft hand, he plucked one of the snakes from around his neck and ran his forefinger down its throat too. It went as limp as the first one. The third cobra got the same treatment.

The snake charmer looked at Jaxon and smiled. "Stand, please."

"Um, I'd rather not, if you don't mind."

"Don't you want to see Moroccan culture?"

"Not like this."

"Then why are you here?"

"I'm looking for people like me."

The old man glanced at one of his snakes as though expressing surprise to a friend and then looked back at Jaxon.

"People with dark skin and blue eyes? The People from the Sea?"

Jaxon perked up. "You know about us?"

"I know much secret knowledge"—he gestured with the limp snakes—"but learning such knowledge always comes at a risk."

"Tell me about it," Jaxon said, thinking about the fight and chase in Chinatown.

"So you understand?" the snake charmer asked.

"Yes," Jaxon said, not really sure what he meant.

"Then stand."

"I told you I don't want to be part of your show."

The snake charmer gave her a wicked grin. "Knowledge comes at a price. My price is danger. Stand and meet my legless friends. Do it without trembling or hesitation, and I will take you to your people."

Jaxon paused, unable to believe what the guy was saying. Did this jerk really want her to risk her life just so he'd take her to the Atlanteans? Why couldn't he just ask for money?

The snake charmer kept his gaze fixed on her. The crowd didn't make a sound. She looked at all the expectant faces around her. When they'd thought she was Moroccan, they hadn't paid attention to her at all. Since they now knew she was a foreigner, all eyes were fixed on her. Did they expect her to run off? The snake charmer certainly thought so. Annoyed, Jaxon rose to her feet.

She cocked her head and studied him. "Go on, do your worst."

The snake charmer cocked his eyebrow again.

"My worst? Oh, that was a foolish thing to say. A very foolish thing, indeed."

Like a single creature, the three snakes lifted themselves erect and stared at her, their tongues flicking in and out. The snake charmer hadn't done a thing to make them do that. It was as though the serpents had been listening to their conversation. The old man gave her a wicked grin and moved his hands forward. The snakes loomed up in her face, their black, inhuman eyes staring into her own.

Chapter 13

July 28, 2016, MARRAKESH, MOROCCO
12:30 P.M.

Jaxon's body went rigid with fear as the snake charmer leaned toward her, the three snakes in his hands extending their bodies to reach for her face.

She jerked a little as the closest one flicked its tongue against her cheek, then she froze as all three got so close they became blurry. Their tongues flicked on her cheeks, her ears, her eyes, and they parted like a spreading hand to coil around her neck.

The snake charmer smiled and let go of the snakes. They hung over her neck and shoulders. She could feel them, but they were too close to see, and she didn't dare turn her head to check what they were doing. She suppressed a shudder, not daring to move.

The snake charmer shouted something in Arabic, raising his hands. The crowd cheered.

"Turn around and face the people," he told her in English. "They admire your bravery, as do I."

"I-I don't want to move."

"I am master of all serpents. They will not hurt you unless I tell them to. Are you afraid?"

"Yes."

"Do you trust me?"

"Um..."

"Allah hates a liar. Do you trust me?"

"No."

"Good. Turn around."

Inch by inch, Jaxon eased her body around to face the crowd, trying not to make any sudden moves or sway her upper body.

As she turned, she saw the faces of the crowd. Everyone was staring at her with wide-eyed wonder. The little girls wore looks of open admiration.

Jaxon straightened her spine a little. She had never seen people looking at her as they were. It was a bit pathetic that she had to have three poisonous cobras draped around her neck and shoulders to get that look, but with her pathetic life, she'd take what she could get.

Pathetic? Life could be a little more pathetic right about now!

A little girl of about six in a white dress and a big bow in her hair said something to her and clapped.

"Don't try this at home, kid," she told the girl.

"It is your people who taught me this art," the snake charmer said.

"That's great. Can you take these snakes off me now and take me to them?"

"Certainly. You have earned it, but you have one more task to perform."

The snake charmer put a shiny brass bowl in her hands.

"Go through the people and collect money."

"How about I just pay you for your trouble, and you take the snakes off me?" Jaxon asked.

"But look, they are all taking money out of their pockets. You would deny them the honor of thanking you?"

"Oh, so I get to keep the money?"

The snake charmer belted out a laugh. He translated for the crowd, and they laughed too. Jaxon blushed.

"You better lead me to my people," Jaxon grumbled, inching forward as the snakes turned their heads to stare at her.

"I swear to Allah that I will. This was only a test to see if you deserved to meet them."

Jaxon moved slowly through the crowd with the bowl held out, keeping it as low as her arm would allow. She didn't want to bend down for those who were still seated. Any sudden movement might upset the snakes. Coins plunked into the bowl, and a few people even put in banknotes. Once she finished, she crept back to the snake charmer, who stood by the fountain with his arms crossed and a smug expression on his face.

"Here's your money. Now take me to my people," Jaxon said, holding out the bowl.

The snake charmer counted the money while Jaxon stood there impatiently, the snakes still draped over her.

Nodding in appreciation, he stuffed the money in his pockets as the crowd dispersed. Almost as an afterthought, he casually plucked the snakes one by one off of her and stuck them in the baskets.

Once they were safely put away, Jaxon rounded on him.

"How could you put me in danger like that!"

The snake charmer gave her a gap-toothed grin. "They would not hurt you. I have them in my control."

"Yeah, but they were on me, not you!"

He spread his hands in a helpless gesture. "The worst they could do is bite you."

"Yeah, and then I would have died."

"Oh no, I removed the poison from them. Each snake has a little sac at the back of its throat. I remove these with a razor."

Jaxon cocked her head. "Really?"

The old man inclined his head. "I may dance with snakes for a living, but I am not stupid." He picked up his baskets and smiled. "I am impressed by you. Many Americans would have run away in fear, not of my snakes so much but of us. Americans do not understand the people here and think we are all terrorists. Unfortunately, there are terrorists among us, so we must be careful. Some people in this country hate the secret knowledge I have learned. Come."

The snake charmer led her down an alley, and Jaxon soon got lost again as they navigated the maze of the medina. After a few minutes, they emerged into another small square, where another entertainer stood in front of an old mosque, performing in front of a crowd.

Peering around the backs of the people standing in front of her, Jaxon gasped. Facing the crowd stood an Atlantean. There was no mistaking—he had the same broad face, the same Asian eyes, and the same brilliant blue eyes set off by black skin. He looked to be in his middle age, but it was hard to tell because he had that weathered, weary look that so many poor people had there.

The Atlantean wore a long robe made up of strips of brightly colored cloth. His head was bare, and long dreadlocks reached past his shoulders. Spread out in front of him on a blanket were innumerable little bottles and jars filled with strange liquids and powders of all colors.

As the Atlantean called out to the crowd, he was mixing the substances in a brass bowl and encouraging people to have a taste. Several people came forward to try his concoction. Soon, money changed hands, and people moved off with samples in little plastic bags.

"His name is Moustafa," the snake charmer said. "He is a healer."

"That stuff is medicine?"

"Most powerful medicine. He can cure anything. Sadly, he cannot cure the war in his own country. He fled here from Mali. Al-Qaeda was killing people like him."

"Killing my people?" Jaxon felt a chill.

"No, most people do not even know your kind are from the sea. That is secret knowledge. They were killing healers like him because they say his medicine is outside of Koranic teachings, a kind of sorcery."

"Is it?"

The snake charmer gave her another of his gap-toothed grins. "That depends on your opinion."

The Atlantean's show ended, and the crowd gradually broke up. He gathered up his powders and liquids in a big steel box covered in Arabic text written in swirly green letters. He spotted the snake charmer and waved to him, putting his hand to his heart. Then he saw Jaxon. His face lit up with interest, and he hurried over, bowing to her and saying something in Arabic.

"Moustafa does not understand English," the snake charmer said. "I will have to translate."

The two men spoke for a while like old friends before the snake charmer turned back to Jaxon.

"Moustafa says he is happy to meet you and that he wants to help you find out more about your people. He regrets he does not know much himself, only some old stories. He came from a small village in the desert and has no education."

"What does he know?"

The snake charmer and Moustafa conferred for a while as Jaxon stood by impatiently, frustrated by the language barrier. Then the snake charmer translated again.

"He says your people came from their island home in the sea long, long ago, centuries before the Romans conquered this land. Their island sank because of the people's sins, and they sailed here, to what is now Morocco. At first, they built cities and tried to keep their old ways, but people from the desert attacked them, as well as warriors from the south in what is now Senegal and Gambia. By the time the Romans came, the People from the Sea had scattered. They were persecuted for their knowledge and magical powers, and they learned to hide. Soon, many forgot about their past, as you have forgotten. Even those who keep the knowledge have lost most of it."

The snake charmer stopped speaking. After a moment, Jaxon realized he was finished.

"That's it?" she asked. That hardly added anything to what they already knew.

"Moustafa apologizes, but he is not an educated man. He comes from Kirchamba, a village near Timbuktu. He says there are scholars in Timbuktu who know much more. Many people wrote down the old stories, and some of these are preserved in ancient manuscripts. You will find out more from the people there."

"How did he learn what he knows?"

"From his parents. Didn't your parents teach you about this?"

Jaxon hung her head. Moustafa said something to her in a sympathetic tone.

"Ah, he understands now," the snake charmer said. "You are an orphan. Sometimes the People from the Sea are not careful, and regular people become afraid of their powers. Ignorant people will sometimes drive them from the village or even stone them to death for witch-craft. The children end up as orphans. Sometimes, the parents will give them up in order to protect them."

Jaxon nodded, feeling her guts twist. Yeah, her parents had been forced to make the same choice. It must have ripped their hearts apart. When she focused again, Moustafa was writing something in Arabic on a slip of paper.

The snake charmer went on. "He lived most of his life in his village, but he spent some years in Timbuktu learning his trade. He's giving you the name and address of a scholar he once knew. He does not know if he is still alive because he was an old man when Moustafa fled in 2012. That was when the terrorists took over the city. They are gone now, but you still must be careful if you go there."

Suddenly, Jaxon had an idea.

"Why don't you come with me back to my hotel? I'm here with some people who are researching the Atlanteans, the People from the Sea, as you call them. They'd love to hear what Moustafa has to say."

When the snake charmer translated this, suddenly Moustafa's entire attitude changed. His face got a guarded look, and he wagged an angry finger at Jaxon as he lectured her in Arabic.

"Moustafa says that no good can come from letting regular people study your people. Even those who start by meaning well end up twisting it to their own ends. You should be very careful of these people."

"They saved my life!"

"Only to claim it for their own. Moustafa does not want to meet them and says you should get away from them."

"They're my friends."

The two men did not look convinced. Moustafa said something.

"He regrets he cannot help you more than he has. He suggests going to Timbuktu and seeing his old friend. There, you will learn more. And now, we must go."

"Wait, you can't leave! You're the first Atlantean I've ever met!"

But they did leave. Moustafa shook her hand, and when Jaxon refused to let go, tears brimming in her eyes, he gave her a warm smile and patted her on the shoulder. Then he reached into his case and produced a small vial of green liquid.

"He says this is his most powerful medicine. If a person is dying, whether from being hurt or getting a disease, it will cure him. But there is only enough to cure one. He says he is sorry, but he must go now. He wishes you luck, and I wish you luck as well. May Allah protect you!"

And with that, they led her back to where she had met the snake charmer and departed. Jaxon trudged back to the hotel, confused and dejected.

The scene back at the hotel was predictable. Edward was there freaking out, actually out of his room and standing in the main courtyard, trembling and soaked with sweat. Everyone else had scattered across the city to search for her.

Jaxon got Edward calmed down enough to call everyone in then led him up to his room, where he could rest. Each member of the Atlantis Allegiance came back one by one, so she got five different chewing-out sessions. Grunt's was the scariest, and Otto's made her feel the guiltiest.

She stood her ground.

"This is my life and my heritage, and I've found out something none of you have. We're meeting in my room in an hour." That was all she would say.

They all met there as she had told them to. Even Edward showed up, still looking exhausted from the daylong panic attack Jaxon had inflicted on him. She would apologize to him later. Right then, those people needed to listen to her.

"I met an Atlantean. His name is Moustafa, and he's some sort of folk healer. He comes from Mali and says there's more of my people down there than there are up here." She turned to the two scientists. "What do you know about that?"

Yamazaki and Yuhle had been seeing some historians and geneticists at Cadi Ayyad University. Yuhle answered her.

"The local experts we've been talking to noticed several years ago that the Atlanteans were a separate people with a long, distinct history. They hadn't made a connection to Atlantis or any special abilities, though."

"Looks like they haven't read any of my articles," Dr. Yamazaki grumbled.

"Where do they think the Atlanteans came from?" Jaxon asked. "The snake charmer who introduced me to them called Atlanteans the 'People from the Sea.'"

Everyone did a double take at her mention of the snake charmer.

Yamazaki looked at her curiously and said, "They admit they don't know. They say the population suddenly appears in the ancient records about three thousand years ago. The thing is, written documentation from that far back is sketchy in this part of the world—only a few monumental inscriptions on the bases of statues and things like that. There is some oral tradition, though, and it says that the population arrived from the sea and became leaders in the ancient settlements here. Of course, empires rise and fall, and there's been a lot of fighting in this region, so eventually the Atlanteans scattered."

"So why would they flee to Mali? Isn't that all desert?" Jaxon asked.

"Most of it is," Grunt replied. "Fighting tends to be around important places like cities and river fords. If you want to run away, going into the Sahara pretty much guarantees you won't be followed."

"So where is Timbuktu, exactly?" Jaxon asked.

"In Mali, to the southeast," Yamazaki said. "Here, let's look at the map." The scientist spread a map out on the table and used a compass to hold it down against the light breeze blowing through the window and ruffling the map's edges. "As you can see, Morocco hugs the northwest coast of Africa. To the east is Algeria. Now, you can see to the south is this country called Mauritania. It's one of the poorest in Africa, and just east of that is Mali. Timbuktu is here, in northern Mali, right in the middle of the Sahara."

"So why would Moustafa tell us Timbuktu is the place to go to learn about my history?" Jaxon asked. "It's so remote."

"It's remote now, but once it was a center of trade for caravans crossing the Sahara. It became a center of learning and culture too. The town has the oldest library in all northwest Africa. There was a university there, starting in the thirteenth century, and lots of families had traditions of being scholars and kept their own private libraries, some handed down over centuries. If any place is going to preserve knowledge of Atlantis, it will be Timbuktu. Silly of me not to think of it before."

"Wait, didn't al-Qaeda take that place a few years ago?" Otto said. "They destroyed a bunch of Muslim shrines."

Yuhle nodded. "Yes, killed a bunch of civilians too. But the locals snuck the books out of the city, and they survived. According to BBC News, they've brought them back. I just read about that a couple of months ago."

Dr. Yamazaki peered at the map. "Judging from the Moroccan studies our colleagues here have been doing, it seems that the further south you go, the more people there are with the Atlantis gene. I'd love to do a regional genetic sample here!"

Grunt laughed. "I don't think the government is going to give you permission to jab a few thousand people for some genetic test. How would you explain it?"

The scientist shook her head. "No, I guess it's impossible. The thing is, though, if Atlanteans are common down in the Sahara, the scholars in Timbuktu would know about them, just like Moustafa said. Maybe they kept some knowledge from ancient times."

"There's only one way to find out. The question is, how best to get there?" Yuhle asked.

Edward spoke for the first time. "I don't think flying would be a good idea. Not many foreigners are flying to Mali these days, thanks to the war, so we might get noticed."

Yamazaki rubbed her chin. "Then it looks like we'll have to drive. The most direct route would be to go straight south, cutting through Algeria, but there's a nasty civil war there, so we have to avoid that. The only other way is to swing around the border then cut southeast through this little bit of northern Mauritania here before getting into Mali. Then we can drive southeast to get to Timbuktu."

Grunt jabbed a thumb in the direction of Otto and Jaxon. "So you want to take our teenage sweethearts into a desert filled with minefields, Islamic militias, an active slave trade, and the occasional suicide bomber thrown in just for chuckles? And you want to do this in the middle of summer? If this is your idea of history homework, I'd hate to see your idea of mixed martial arts."

Dr. Yamazaki grinned. "Do you want to learn the secret to Atlantis or not?"

"I'm more into killing General Meade and his goons before they overthrow America. But this will piss him off, so I'm in," Grunt said.

"Wait." Otto held up a hand. "So this place is still dangerous? I thought the terrorists were gone."

"Gone out of the city," Vivian said. "There are still plenty of them in the region. They blow up bombs in the main cities sometimes, too. Plus, both Mauritania and Mali have rebel groups trying to overthrow the government or separate some of the provinces into their own countries. Some of these groups are fundamentalists who pledge allegiance to Al-Qaeda and ISIS—some aren't. None of them would really be happy having us drive through their territory."

Otto and Jaxon stared at each other. After a moment, they turned back to the rest of the Atlantis Allegiance.

"So no one else has a problem with this?" Jaxon asked.

Dr. Yuhle chuckled, adjusting his glasses. "I think we all have a problem with it. I just don't see any other way we're going to learn what we're after."

"I don't want to put Jaxon in danger," Otto said. "It's too risky."

Jaxon frowned at him. "Hello? That's my decision."

"But it's crazy!"

Jaxon paused. Yeah, it was crazy. She was objecting to Otto speaking for her, not what he'd actually said. It really was too risky.

She looked at the map, studying the unfamiliar names and the vast empty spaces in between. The compass at the edge of the map made an appropriate symbol. She felt like some old-school explorer. This was a dangerous part of the world to explore, though.

And that was the temptation. She'd seen so much already, all the hints and clues that didn't quite add up but pointed in the right direction. She was getting close to finding out the truth about herself. She could sense it.

The idea of going to Timbuktu made her heart race and her skin go cold. She'd seen plenty of news reports of Iraq and Syria. If Mali was anything like that...

"I'll go," she said.

Jaxon felt a delicious spike of anticipation, a surge of adrenaline. It was that same wonderful feeling she'd gotten when she waited for Brett so they could go hunting in the bad parts of LA. It made her feel awake and alive, as if she were at the center of the universe. Her senses intensified, and colors seemed brighter and sounds clearer.

She'd had that ever since she'd gotten here, but the thought of going farther into the unknown, really pushing her luck and doing something she would have never pictured herself doing a few weeks ago, made her feel ten feet tall.

Everyone was staring at her, jaws slack.

She laughed. "What, did you expect me to say no? You got the wrong girl!"

She waved the compass at Vivian. "You're going to have to show me how to use this. It looks like I'm going to be a world traveler before this is all over."

Jaxon froze. The compass was in her hand.

She hadn't picked it up.

Dr. Yamazaki pointed a trembling finger at the compass. "Have you ever moved objects before, moved them from a distance?"

Jaxon licked her lips, embarrassed, like some sort of sideshow being stared at in a circus. "Um, yeah."

"Why didn't you tell us?" Yuhle asked. "We even tested you for that power."

Jaxon shrugged. "It kind of freaks me out."

She glanced at Otto, who had edged away and was looking at her with wide eyes.

"Plus, I don't want people thinking I'm a freak."

"No one thinks that, Jaxon," Otto said, looking embarrassed. "We just need to find out more. Even the scientists don't have any real answers to all these questions."

"All the more reason to go ask the experts in Timbuktu," she said.

Otto shook his head. "It's too risky."

"Don't go, then," Jaxon snapped.

He looked her in the eye. "I go where you go."

Yamazaki leaned over the table to peer at her. "Could you move another object, please? Here, let me lay out some objects of different weights, and we'll see how much you can move."

"We should try it from different distances too," Yuhle said, helping her lay out a pen, a lighter, a pair of binoculars, and a bottle of water on the table. "I'll get my notebook and take down the readings."

Jaxon raised her hands, suddenly annoyed. "Wait! I'm not some lab rat. I'm sick of these tests."

The two scientists stared at her as though she was speaking some strange foreign language.

"But this is important data," Yuhle said.

"I'm not a lab rat," Jaxon repeated, "and I'm sick of being treated like one. If we want to find out about my people, let's find out from my people. Those old manuscripts will have the answer."

Otto looked at her nervously. "So we're going to Timbuktu?"

Jaxon took a deep breath, her heart racing. "Yeah, it looks like we are."

Chapter 14

July 28, 2016, LANGLEY AIR FORCE
BASE, VIRGINIA

3:45 P.M.

General Meade had decided to grab
the lion by the tail. He flew to Virginia,
planning to show up at General Corbin's
office unannounced. He'd called in sick to
work and paid for a civilian flight instead
of taking one of the many military planes
that flew between bases every day,
just in case Corbin was monitoring his
movements.

Now he was driving a rental car up
to the gate of Langley Air Force Base,
where Corbin served as commander. It
was actually a joint base with the US
Army's Fort Eustis, which made it one of

the biggest military bases in the world. It included several jet-fighter squadrons, bomber squadrons, an intelligence unit, and several thousand infantry soldiers. Corbin commanded all of it.

If he wanted to overthrow the government and could get his troops to support him, he could strike at Washington, only three hours away by car and about fifteen minutes by air. No major military installations lay between him and the nation's capital. Corbin was a knife poised to strike at the soft underbelly of the nation's democratic institutions.

General Meade fumed as he drove up to the gate. To think he had toyed with the idea of joining that traitor! He'd been fooled, just like so many others had been fooled, into believing there was a greater danger facing the country, one that justified suspending the will of the people. Meade felt embarrassed that he had been duped and deeply ashamed that he had gone so far down the road to treason.

Well, he would change that. He was going to get to the bottom of this. He would confront Corbin, and if the man didn't give him all the right answers,

Meade would arrest him for treason. The nation needed to be secure against people like Corbin.

After Meade's ID got him through the front gate, he drove to the main parking lot near the administration building where Corbin had his office. At the main entrance, Meade had to show his ID and pass through a metal detector. The general put his keys, phone, and coins on a tray and passed through. The detector didn't beep. The guards nodded and gave him back his things. They didn't notice the slight lump his firearm made in his side pocket.

One of the many pieces of equipment in the Poseidon Project laboratory was a 3D printer. General Meade had the specs for a plastic gun. The government had banned printing such a gun or even owning the program to make it, but there were larger issues at stake. Meade wasn't about to go into the lion's den unarmed. The gun was a fully functional .45 automatic with an eight-round clip of high-density ceramic bullets, undetectable to metal detectors.

Fully armed and ready to shoot General Corbin if necessary, Meade walked down the hall past officers hurrying to their daily tasks. He followed the signs to the high-command wing of the sprawling building, passed through another metal detector with no trouble, and announced himself to Corbin's orderly.

The orderly, a shifty-looking major who looked Meade up and down without meeting his eye, said in a brusque manner, "I don't see you on the appointment list, sir."

The "sir" came out weak, almost as an afterthought.

"Tell him I'm here. He'll see me."

The major made a call. After talking for a moment in a low voice, he put down the phone and studied Meade for a moment. "The general will see you now, sir."

Meade was ushered into Corbin's office. The general, a lean Vietnam War veteran with deepening lines on his face, gave Meade a firm handshake.

"Good to see you again, Hector. This is a surprise," Corbin said.

Meade waited until Corbin dismissed his orderly, asking him to close the door behind him. Corbin quietly locked it.

"We'll go for a walk in a minute," Corbin said. Like Meade, he did not trust the military enough to have frank conversations in any building—they were all probably bugged. "Take a seat. Want some coffee?"

"All right," Meade said, sitting down in front of Corbin's desk. Best to bide his time and put Corbin at ease. Meade's hand rested near the hidden pistol.

Corbin went over to a little kitchenette on one side of his office and opened up an Italian stovetop coffeemaker. Filling the bottom steel container with water, he scooped out some ground coffee from a bag into a central pan then screwed on the top, which had the handle and spout. He turned on the stovetop.

"We'll go for a walk in a minute. I'd like you to see our new football field. Just got it finished. How have you been?"

They chatted about trivialities for a couple of minutes. Meade understood what he was doing. Corbin wanted to lull the suspicions of anyone listening in. That made sense, and Meade would generally agree, but he wanted people to be listening in. He wanted someone to hear what he was about to say. Still, he waited as he needed to catch Corbin off guard.

The water boiled up from the bottom of the coffeemaker, through the central pan, and into the top container. Meade had seen those fancy coffeemakers before but had never used one. Regular American pot coffee was good enough for him. A rich aroma filled the room. Corbin switched off the stovetop and filled two cups. Meade watched carefully to make sure he didn't slip anything into one of them. He wouldn't have put it past Corbin to try to poison him.

But perhaps he was wrong. Perhaps Corbin had been duped, too. Meade had to tread carefully.

Corbin handed one of the cups to Meade.

Meade took a sip. It was rich and flavorful and smelled heavenly. In fact, it was the best coffee he had ever tasted.

"Like it?" Corbin asked, sitting down behind his desk. "It's Ethiopian. I buy it from a distributor direct from the country. I was stationed in Ethiopia for a time. I can't share the details of my mission, but while I was there, I got hooked on the coffee. The Ethiopians discovered coffee, you know. Centuries ago. They have a legend about it. Once, there was a goatherd named Kaldi. He noticed that when his goats ate red berries from a certain bush, they'd get all excited, jumping around like crazy. Well, Kaldi tried some of the berries himself and got all jumpy too. He showed some of the berries to a monk who lived nearby, but the monk through they were unholy and threw them in the fire. Then the monk smelled the scent of the roasting beans inside the coffee berries and got tempted. He and Kaldi ground up some of the beans, put them in water, and drank the first cup of coffee. Of course, the monk decided they weren't unholy after all. A fun little story. Who knows? Maybe it's true. We live in a strange world, and it's hard to know what's the truth and what's simply legend."

The two generals locked eyes. For a moment, there was silence. Meade took another gulp to fortify himself and spoke.

"Yes, I've been trying to figure out some legends lately. I'm thinking one that I believed in might not be true after all."

"Oh?" Corbin inclined his head.

"Yes. Since you're fond of traditions, I suppose you know the old saying 'a picture is worth a thousand words.' Now, I'm beginning to think it's worth a thousand lies."

General Corbin smiled. "And what do you mean by that?"

"I mean all those reconnaissance photos of UFOs are faked."

To Meade's surprise, Corbin didn't react at all to that.

Meade went on. "Do you know the name Oscar Preston? He was an intelligence analyst, working on the UFO photos. Top man in that department, and even he was fooled for years. The photos are brilliantly faked, but someone slipped up, and Oscar spotted it. He came to me. Someone shot him. Then they tried to kill me."

Meade pulled the automatic from his pocket and pointed it at General Corbin.

"And you know all about it. I can see it in your eyes."

General Corbin smiled, completely unfazed by the .45 caliber pistol pointed at his face from across the desk. He casually took a sip from his coffee and said, "There's an old quote from Hermann Goering, the head of the Luftwaffe in Nazi Germany, that's always stuck with me. He said, 'Of course the people don't want war. Why should some poor slob on a farm want to risk his life in a war when the best he can get out of it is to come back to his farm in one piece? Naturally, the common people don't want war, neither in Russia, nor in England, nor for that matter in Germany. That is understood. But, after all, it is the leaders of the country who determine the policy, and it is always a simple matter to drag the people along, whether it is a democracy or a fascist dictatorship or a parliament or a communist dictatorship. Voice or no voice, the people can always be brought to the bidding of the leaders. That is easy. All you have to do is tell them they are being attacked and denounce the peacemakers for lack of patriotism and exposing the country to danger. It works the same in any country.'

"Goering was only half right. What he didn't know, what he couldn't predict, was the modern information society. People have too much information now. They can access ideas from the other side. Look at those idiots who have never been outside the States who are pledging themselves to ISIS. Or the American fans of Vladimir Putin. It's hard to have an external enemy when people can learn all about their propaganda with a click on their phone. This country is slipping, Hector. It's slipping because we are no longer unified. We have all these different groups, all these different agendas. Instead of paying attention to a few major sources of information that we can easily control, the newspapers and television, now the more intelligent among the American people are getting information from sources all around the world or even creating their own news sources."

Meade shifted in his seat, keeping the gun held steadily at Corbin's forehead. Why was this man saying all this in his office? Had he found and disabled the bugs?

Corbin went on. "External enemies aren't enough to keep the country together anymore. The center cannot hold. We run the risk of losing our place at the top. What we need is a new kind of external enemy, one that can't be talked to—one that doesn't have websites or Twitter or podcasts—an enemy that's frightening enough to unify people but who will remain silent."

"So you invented an alien invasion," Meade said.

Corbin shrugged. "A lot of people believe in aliens already. And we have experimental craft that look like UFOs, so we can create sightings if we need to. So far, the photos are enough, but sooner or later, we'll have to launch some attacks to get the country unified. And then I'll make this country greater than it ever was."

"General Corbin, I'm arresting you for high treason. If you make a move, I will shoot you." General Meade stood up. He barely made it upright before his head swam, and he had to grab the arm of his chair to steady himself.

Corbin smiled. "I saw you watching me as I poured the coffee to make sure I didn't slip you a mickey. What you couldn't know was that I brushed some transparent tranquilizer onto the inside of your cup before you even entered my office. I knew I was dealing with a cautious man."

Corbin ducked under his desk just as General Meade pulled the trigger. The bullet punched a hole in the back wall. Staggering past the desk, using one hand to support himself, General Meade tried to come around to take another shot.

He only made it three steps before slumping to the floor, unconscious.

* * *

General Meade didn't know how long he'd been out. His first emotion was surprise that he had woken up at all.

All he could see was a hazy light. That slowly resolved itself into an overhead fluorescent lamp.

Meade turned his head and tried to focus his eyes. Lab equipment stood all around him. A heart monitor sat next to the operating table on which he lay. It pulsed with a steady beat, showing his vital signs. He tried to move his arms and legs but found himself strapped down.

Looking around again, he thought the place looked familiar. As the cobwebs cleared from his mind, he realized why.

He was in the laboratory of the Poseidon Project.

General Corbin strode into view. Dr. Jones, the lead researcher of the Poseidon Project, came timidly behind him.

"Glad to see you're awake, Hector," Corbin said. "I must admit, you caught me by surprise with that plastic pistol. That's something I didn't anticipate. Good thing my office is soundproofed. Covering up the bullet hole was a pain in the ass, though. Luckily, the bullet embedded itself in a support beam and didn't fly right into poor Colonel Maxwell's office. That would have been hard to explain. He's not on board with us. You're resourceful—I'll grant you that. But you're inefficient. You've had months to catch the Atlantis Allegiance, and you couldn't even hold onto a sixteen-year-old girl. There's far too much at stake for you to stay in charge of this operation.

"Oh, you didn't realize I've been monitoring your operation all along? As you probably suspected, I planted that Roswell report so you'd get in touch. It was time to consolidate the operation. Unfortunately for you, we're going to have to consolidate it a bit more than I previously anticipated. Dr. Jones, the needles please."

The scientist moved forward, looking embarrassed. Meade glared at him, and the scientist blushed. Then Jones turned to the right, where Meade saw another operating table. A teenage boy lay on it, unconscious. After a moment, Meade recognized him from a surveillance image in his files—Brett Lawson, Jaxon's boyfriend who had disappeared on one of her nocturnal outings. He had figured, as had the Grants, that he had been killed.

"Do you recognize this young gentleman?" Corbin asked. "I had some of my agents kidnap him and fake a police report. I wanted to push her a little further down the road to violence. I know that you were planning on pushing her the same way, but you wouldn't have had the nerve to do something like this. You're too weak, Hector, which is why we're going to have to work on you."

Dr. Jones wiped Brett's arm and injected him with something.

"What are you doing to him?" General Meade asked, his voice coming out slurred.

"The same thing we're going to do to you. You see, Dr. Jones here has been doing some research on the side without your knowledge. Research for me. He thinks he's isolated a way to give Atlantean powers to regular human beings. He tried to explain it to me, but I've never had much of a scientific bent. Something about replicating the enzymes in their systems. He's warned me that it could kill you and Brett, but I figure that's worth the risk. If it succeeds, then you both will be valuable tools. If it fails…" General Corbin gave a little shrug.

Dr. Jones approached with a hypodermic in his hand.

"You'll never get away with this," Meade growled.

General Corbin laughed as the scientist wiped Meade's arm and injected him with his serum. "But Hector, I already have! Don't worry, soon you'll be working for the dictator of the most powerful nation on Earth."

Chapter 15

AUGUST 1, 2016, IN THE DESERT
NEAR AIN BEN TILI, ON THE
BORDER BETWEEN MOROCCO AND
MAURITANIA

3:45 P.M.

Illegally crossing an international border into a war zone turned out to be easier than Jaxon had thought. Grunt and Otto had picked up a pair of Land Rovers filled with camping gear and a few heavy duffel bags they didn't want to talk about, and as the muezzin called the dawn prayer, the Atlantis Allegiance left their secret hotel in the back streets of Marrakesh and headed south. Vivian, Otto, and Jaxon rode in one vehicle while

Grunt and the scientists rode in the other.

Edward stayed at the hotel. Flying across the Atlantic to a strange country had been as much as he could take. A desert journey to a frontier town was asking too much of him. He kept in contact via a secure Darknet satellite uplink to two computers in the Land Rovers.

The first day was a beautiful drive up winding mountain passes between the jagged peaks of the Atlas Mountains. Otto and Jaxon held hands and stared out the window at all the little villages with their shepherd boys tending herds of goats and sheep. Men tended narrow fields in lush valleys fed by mountain springs, and women sat knitting at the doorways of crude concrete homes or fetched water from village wells.

Jaxon noticed all the villages lay tucked into the little valleys made by folds in the mountainsides that caught the water. The steep slopes and crags were all but barren of vegetation, and she saw no one there.

The road was better than she expected, a two-lane highway with not too many potholes. Traffic was bad, though, and Vivian had to keep swerving to avoid reckless drivers or eighteen-wheelers straddling the median. Jaxon couldn't blame them. Most of the hairpin turns didn't have guardrails and looked out over sickening thousand-foot drops. Otto clutched her hand a little more tightly on those.

They took most of the day to get over the mountains before the land flattened out into a barren, gritty desert. Vivian explained they were approaching the true Sahara, the huge band of sand dunes that ran across the entire African continent from the Atlantic Ocean to the Red Sea. That night, they camped under the stars on a dirt road without a village in sight. The Atlantis Allegiance had learned to be careful.

The next day, they entered the Sahara Desert. The road was still two lanes, but it became gravel and ran through long stretches of featureless sand dunes. Once they came across a military checkpoint, where bored, lean soldiers toting assault rifles studied the papers Edward had provided for them, asked a few questions, and let them pass.

Shortly after the checkpoint, Grunt and Vivian steered the Land Rovers off the road and struck out across the desert.

"Do you know where we're going?" Jaxon asked Vivian.

"Don't worry, honey," Vivian said, her hands gripping the steering wheel as she maneuvered between sand dunes. "We have to be off-road for a while. There's a Moroccan army base a few miles south of here at the border. We need to avoid it."

"And once we're in Mauritania, what then?"

"Avoid everyone until we get into Mali."

"Will we make it today?" Jaxon asked.

"Nope. Hope you don't mind camping in a war zone."

"Oh sure, we don't mind at all!" Otto laughed, patting one of the heavy duffel bags.

Jaxon frowned at him. "Are there guns in there?"

Otto grinned at her. "Of course. Want one?"

"No. Please don't turn into a gun nut."

Otto's face darkened. "I'm not too happy about having to tote a gun either, but I don't want you captured by Al-Qaeda or some slave traders. Did you know slavery still exists in Mauritania? Edward showed me a report about it. Sickening."

"Lovely. How long until we get out of here and into Mali?"

Vivian answered that. "Late tomorrow at the best. The terrain is pretty rough. It would be quicker if we could take the roads, but we can't."

"You see?" Otto said. "And it won't get any better once we get into Mali. Timbuktu is all right, but Grunt told me there are Al-Qaeda fighters all through northern Mali. Grunt has been training me. You'll be okay."

"I can take care of myself," Jaxon said, pulling her hand away.

She caught Vivian looking at her in the rearview mirror. Jaxon frowned and looked out the window.

For hours, they drove through featureless wasteland—up one side of a sand dune and down the other, again and again for miles. Sometimes, the desert would flatten out, and they sped along a gritty surface of stones and sand. Vivian constantly checked the GPS to make sure they were going the right way. They saw no one, no sign of life.

They only stopped once so that Vivian could refill the gas tank from one of the jerry cans strapped to the roof. Grunt pulled up behind her and did the same. Jaxon got out to stretch her legs.

The instant she opened the door, a wall of heat slammed into her. She took a deep breath through burning nostrils and steadied herself against the side of the car as her head spun.

After a moment, she got adjusted and walked a few steps away from the Land Rovers.

It reminded her of the California heat wave of 2006 when she was a kid. Temperatures had reached 115 degrees. Schools had closed. When her foster parents at the time had tried to take her for a ride somewhere, Jaxon had passed out on the driveway halfway between the front door and the car.

This felt worse.

"Don't go too far," Grunt called to her.

"I won't, trust me."

Jaxon trudged up a nearby sand dune and looked out over the bleak landscape. So this was the famous Sahara Desert. She had imagined camels and oases with palm trees. All she saw was wasteland. How could anyone live here, and why did so many groups want to fight over it?

Boots crunched in the sand behind her. Otto climbed up the sand dune to join her.

"Hey," he said.

"Hey."

They looked out over the desert for a time.

"We okay?" Otto asked.

Jaxon shrugged, not looking at him.

"What's the matter?" Otto asked.

"I don't know. You've been acting all weird. Like you're some big mercenary or something."

"This is my new life now. It's not like I chose it. General Meade's goons keep chasing us. Two months ago, I had never heard a shot fired in anger, and now I've been in a bunch of gunfights."

Jaxon turned and looked at him. "You haven't killed anyone, have you?"

Otto shook his head, still staring out at the horizon. "No. I don't want to. I'm not sure I have a choice, though. If someone comes at me, it's me or them, and I know who I'll choose."

"That sounds like Grunt talking."

"So what?" Otto replied, suddenly angry. "He knows what he's doing. He's saved me and you more than once."

"It just doesn't fit you. Even in that messed-up group home, you were the nicest, most grounded guy around."

Otto snorted. "Yeah, grounded. I'm addicted to lighting fires."

"Yeah, and Grunt won't let you forget it. Why does he always call you Pyro?"

"Because he's annoying. He means well, though. I think he does it so I won't forget. Keep me from slipping up again."

"You really look up to him, don't you?"

Otto nodded. "He's kinda like a big brother now. That's cool. I never had a real family."

"Tell me about it," Jaxon grumbled.

"You know Edward offered to help me get in touch with my parents? He said I could write a letter to them telling them I'm safe, and he could send it by some special courier, no questions asked. The courier would mail it from the United States so it would look like I was in Alabama or Ohio or somewhere."

"What did you tell them?"

Otto shrugged. "I didn't write them."

"Why not? They must be worried sick about you."

Otto sighed. "No, I'm sure they're not. That's what everyone is saying, but they don't get it because they had real parents. They can never understand. Neither can you, because you never knew your parents so you romanticize them. I know it must be tough to be an orphan, but trust me when I tell you it's not any easier having parents who don't give a damn."

"Someone else said the same thing to me a while back," Jaxon said, thinking of Brett. "But he was crazy too, just like me—just like you."

"None of those counselors or group homes ever helped us out, and now look where we are. We have to keep all this from making us crazier."

Jaxon kissed him on the cheek. "Yeah, we're going to need a lot of luck with that."

Otto turned and kissed her full on the mouth, and they fell into each other's arms and kissed again.

There was a loud hiss above them as a flaming red ball flew over their heads. Both ducked.

"Come on, lovebirds!" Grunt shouted at them from the Land Rover, waving a flare gun over his head. "Time to hit the road! Hey, Pyro! Did you light her fire? Get it? Light her fire? Ha ha ha ha!"

Grunt and Vivian gave each other a high five and got back into the Land Rovers.

Jaxon rolled her eyes. "Maybe we're the only sane ones here."

The two Land Rovers drove across the desert for the rest of the day. All the landscape looked the same. Sometimes, Jaxon checked the GPS just to reassure herself they were actually moving.

As the sun slanted low on the western horizon, Vivian pulled the Land Rover to a stop. Grunt stopped a few yards behind them.

"We need to fill up again already?" Otto asked.

Vivian started collecting her things. "No. Sunset is only an hour away, so we'll camp here for the night. We don't want to camp too close to the border with Mali. There are army patrols and rebel groups, not to mention smugglers. We don't want to meet any of them."

They started unpacking the gear and setting up the tents. Grunt and Otto were staying in one while the two scientists struggled to erect another. Vivian and Jaxon put up a third. Jaxon noticed that all the tents were positioned almost a hundred yards from each other. When she asked why, Vivian gave a sad smile.

"That's in case we get bombed. With the tents far apart, fewer of us will get hurt."

"Bombed?"

"From the air, we look just like a terror cell hiding out in the desert. The US Air Force has drones all over this area. They might mistake us for some of the bad guys and decide to wipe us out."

"Great, the first time I leave the States, and I might get blown up by the American military."

Jaxon finished staking the last peg in her tent, thinking how she had never been camping before, but there she was in the middle of the Sahara Desert, worrying about missiles falling from the sky. She was beginning to miss Hidden Hills Academy. Even seeing Courtney every day would be easier.

But in a strange way, this was actually kind of fun. The thrill of danger she had felt when prowling bad neighborhoods with Brett was a constant feeling. She felt more awake, more alive. Instead of slumping through her depressing daily routine, she was seeing places she thought she'd never get to and doing things she never thought she could.

They hauled gear into the tents, including sleeping bags for the surprisingly cold nights, some jugs of water, the next day's clothes, and a survival pack Vivian always kept with her.

"Got anything in there to keep the missiles away?" Jaxon asked.

"No. Sure you don't want to share a tent with Otto? Might be your last chance."

"Very funny. Do all soldiers make jokes about dying?"

"It's called gallows humor, and yes we do," Vivian said. "It keeps us sane."

"Sane. Right."

They arranged the interior of the tent as they had the previous night. Jaxon found it odd that they did it the exact same way they had the last time—Jaxon's sleeping bag on the left, Vivian's on the right. The survival pack was placed at their heads. Their feet pointed toward the opening of the tent. Their spare clothing was piled between them, creating a little wall and the illusion of privacy. They had already fallen into a routine. As with her morning practices in the secret hotel, routine seemed important in a strange situation. Vivian obviously believed that too, and from the little Jaxon knew of her life, she was always in strange situations. Maybe having a little bit of predictability in a chaotic life was important.

Once they finished, Jaxon sat down and turned on her tablet. One good thing about being with that band of lunatics was that she had access to technology again. Edward had filled her tablet with movies and games, enough to keep her entertained for months. That was a bit of normal, Western life she clung to. She might have been sitting in a tent in the middle of the desert in Africa, but at least she could catch up on her favorite series. Thanks to the Grants, she was way behind. She laughed at the irony. Because of their weird ideas, she actually had even more to entertain her.

She tapped on an episode of her favorite comedy show. Those days, she wasn't in the mood for anything heavy—too much real-life drama. Vivian sat beside her, looking at herself with a small mirror while combing her hair. How that woman managed to stay so beautiful so easily in that place was a bit of a mystery.

"Ugh, what's going on?" Vivian grumbled a few minutes later.

Jaxon looked at her and saw strands of her blond hair standing on end. No matter how much Vivian tried to brush it, static electricity kept pulling some hair up to almost touch the canvas of the tent.

"Maybe it's because it's so dry?" Jaxon gestured toward the tent opening.

As she did, she happened to move her hand too close to Vivian's, and there was a loud snap as they both got a shock.

Vivian and Jaxon laughed, but the laugh didn't last long. They both became aware of a prickly sensation all over their bodies. The dry air crackled with static electricity. Jaxon touched the side of the tent and jerked her hand back as little arcs of electricity passed from the canvas to her fingertips. For a moment, she thought she had discovered another power, but then Vivian cursed, her sleeping bag making crackling noises and lighting up inside as she crawled out of it, creating a series of pops that sounded as if she was making popcorn inside it.

"What's going on?" Jaxon asked.

"Bad news." Vivian grasped the tent's zipper and winced as it gave her a loud shock. Wisps of her blond hair still stood on end, drawn to the top of the tent like feelers. She opened the tent, and they stared out.

The door to the nearest Land Rover slammed shut. Inside, Grunt and Otto were gesturing at them to come over. Beyond that, they saw Yuhle and Yamazaki hurrying to the second Land Rover, but Jaxon barely noticed them. What she saw farther away captured her full attention.

There was lurid yellow light on the horizon, and a sound like dull thunder rumbled in her ears. The horizon looked strange, too thick, and Jaxon needed a moment to realize what she was seeing.

A sickly yellow cloud was rapidly thickening as it approached. The light dimmed as if someone had turned down a lamp. Jaxon glanced up at the sun and saw it half obscured, the sky turning a gritty blue.

"Sandstorm!" Vivian pushed Jaxon back inside and zipped up the tent.

"Wait, wouldn't we be safer in the Land Rover?"

"No time."

The words barely got out of Vivian's mouth before there was a loud rasping sound on the tent as if someone was rubbing it with a giant piece of sandpaper. A hard wind flailed at the canvas, snapping the sides inward and lashing at the two women. They huddled closer together in the center of the bucking and swaying tent.

"What do we do?" Jaxon shouted over the howling wind.

"Sit here and try not to die!"

"Shouldn't we get into the Land Rover?"

"We wouldn't make it five yards, honey. It's better to stay here. You sank the tent pegs in pretty good. Don't worry, the tent probably won't blow over."

The way she said that made Jaxon think something worse was in store.

The wind picked up, the sides of the tent flapping back and forth like a sail on a stormy sea. Vivian and Jaxon sat right in the middle of the tent so they wouldn't get slapped by the flapping canvas. The interior dimmed. When they'd first entered the tent, the sides glowed with the late afternoon light. Now, they turned dull brown then pitch black. The only light came from Jaxon's tablet. Television characters cracked jokes while a laugh track played in the background.

Slowly, Jaxon became aware of another sound, a low hiss that came from all around them. It steadily rose in volume until it sounded like a blaring radio tuned between stations. The sides of the tent no longer flapped but bowed inward, practically touching the two frightened occupants as they clutched each other in the center. After a moment, Jaxon realized what the sound was—sand rasping against the canvas.

"What do we do?" Jaxon asked, having to shout to be heard over the sandstorm.

"Nothing we can do, honey. Just sit tight and hope for the best."

Then came the longest wait of Jaxon's life. They sat there, listening to the rasp of the sand and the howling of the wind as the comedy show chattered on in the background. The tent sides sagged down as sand piled up against them. Vivian and Jaxon pushed against them to move the sand away, only to have to do it again a couple minutes later. Each time, it grew harder and harder as more and more sand piled up all around them.

"We better hope this blows over soon, or we'll get buried!" Vivian shouted over the sound of the storm.

"Maybe we should risk getting out of the tent."

"Not a good option. Only if the tent collapses." Vivian pulled a Bowie knife out of her bag. "Take this. I have another. If the tent falls down, we'll have to cut our way out. Get on top of the sand, curl yourself up into a ball, and hope for the best."

The two women sat there, still pushing on the sides of the tent to try to keep the sand off. Soon, they were crushed into a little corner of the tent, the rest of it flattened by the weight of the dune forming on top of them.

Just as Jaxon was getting ready to slash the canvas and get out of there, the hiss of blowing sand lessened, and the top of the tent lightened as sunlight poked through the murk.

Within a few minutes, the wind died down and the light came back, as strong as before.

Jaxon and Vivian sighed in relief. Using their feet, they pushed away a big lump of sand in front of the tent entrance and unzipped the flap. A heap of sand poured in, covering most of their gear. They clambered over it and out. Jaxon looked back and saw only about a third of the tent poking out from the surface. Beyond it, the yellow cloud of the sandstorm was quickly receding into the distance.

Then she turned to look at the rest of the camp.

She couldn't see it.

The other two tents, the Land Rovers, the campfire Yuhle had been preparing— all were gone, replaced with featureless sand dunes.

Slowly, Jaxon turned 360 degrees. There was nothing... nothing but sand for hundreds of miles. The rest of the Atlantis Allegiance had disappeared, and they were alone in the Sahara Desert.

About the Author

S.A. Beck lives in sunny California. When she's not surfing, knitting or daydreaming in a hammock, she's writing novels.